The Weatherman. Vol. 2

CREATORS: JODY LEHEUP AND NATHAN FOX

WRITER: JODY LEHEUP
ARTIST: NATHAN FOX
COLORIST: MORENO DINISIO
LETTERER: STEVE WANDS
DESIGNER: TOM MULLER
EDITOR: JOSH JOHNS

COVER: NATHAN FOX

SPECIAL THANKS: ROBERT LEHEUP AND SEBASTIAN GIRNER

PRODUCTION ARTIST: DEANNA PHELPS
NATHAN FOX HAND LETTERED FONT DESIGN: JOHN GREEN

Originally published as THE WEATHERMAN Vol. 2 #1–6

PREVIOUSLY:

Local weatherman Nathan Bright was living the good life on terraformed Mars when he's suddenly accused of carrying out the worst terrorist attack in human history—an attack that killed billions of people on Earth.

Confused, terrified, and hunted by the entire galaxy, Nathan's only hope lies with government agent Amanda Cross, who informs Nathan that he isn't Nathan Bright at all. His real name is Ian Black and he's a member of the Sword of God, the notorious terrorist group responsible for the attack.

Nathan doesn't remember any of this because Ian Black wiped his mind and gave himself a new identity as Nathan Bright. Why he did so remains a mystery...

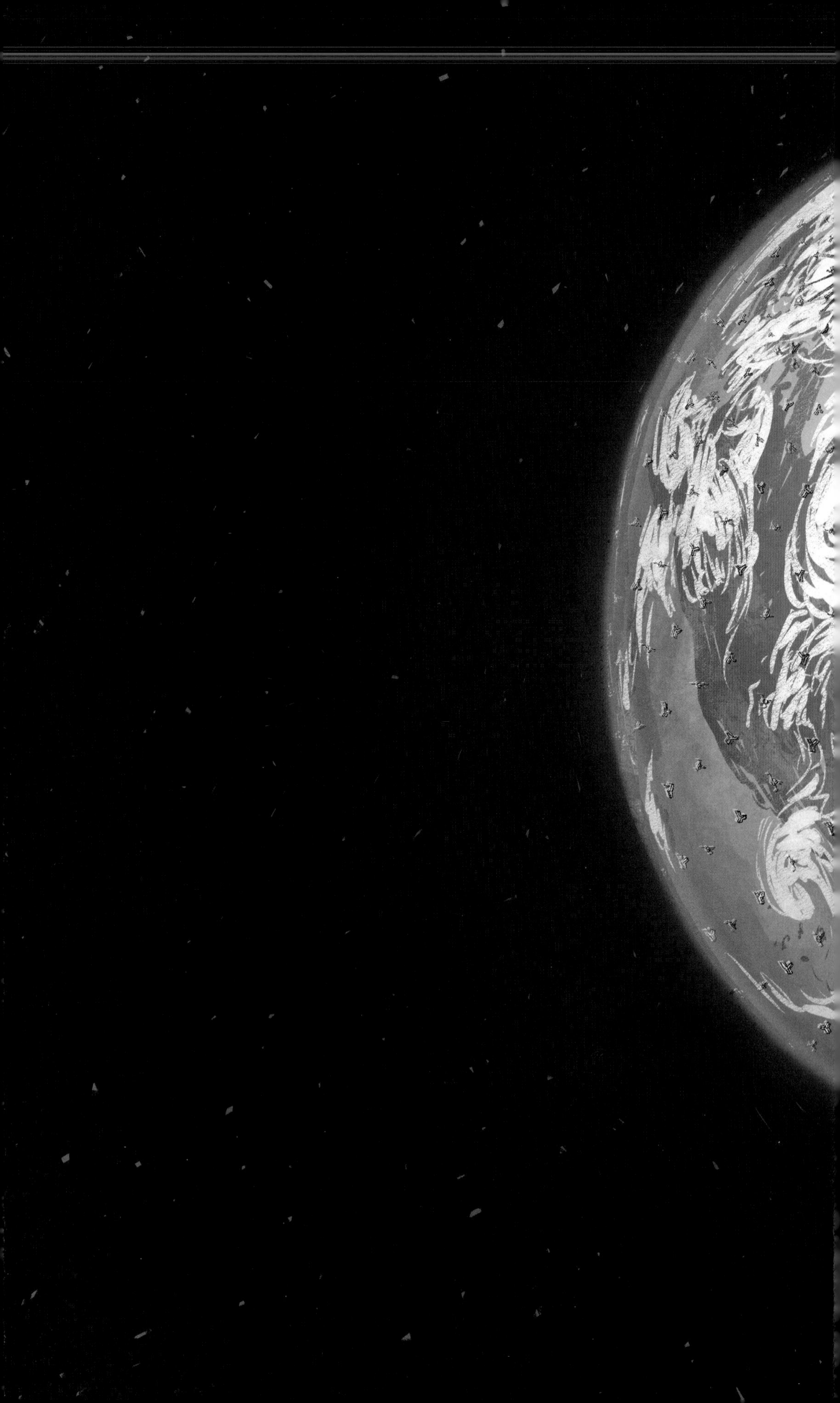

GODDAMNIT, CETH.

STOP!
WARNING
DANGER!
WHAT?
WE'VE BEEN REASSIGNED TO *SPACE-SIDE,* THAT'S WHAT!

I LIKE SPACE-SIDE.
YEAH RIGHT.
I KNOW YOU DO, CETH. BECAUSE YOU'RE SIMPLE. BUT I'M A MAN OF *ACTION.* I HAVE A RIGOROUS MIND.
I NEED *STIMULATION.*

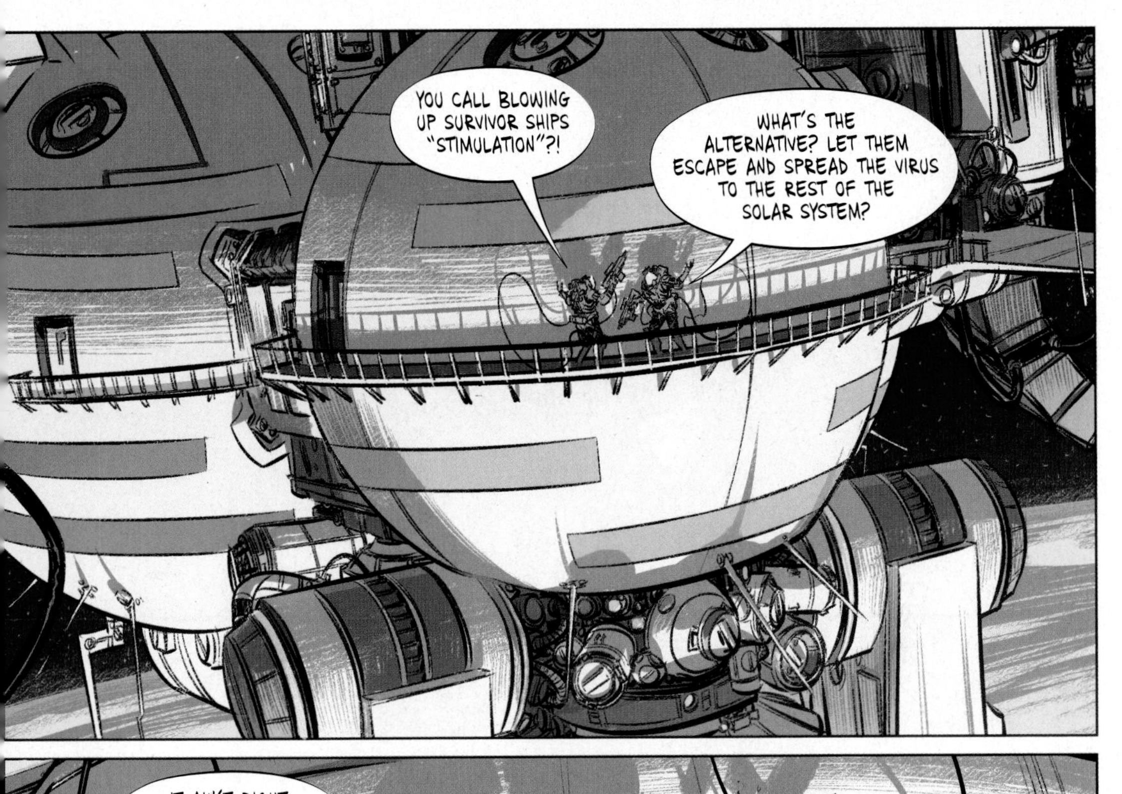
YOU CALL BLOWING UP SURVIVOR SHIPS "STIMULATION"?!
WHAT'S THE ALTERNATIVE? LET THEM ESCAPE AND SPREAD THE VIRUS TO THE REST OF THE SOLAR SYSTEM?

IT AIN'T RIGHT, THAT'S ALL I'M SAYIN'. MAYBE THERE'S ANOTHER WAY TO--
OH GOOD, WELL, WE'LL JUST *HAVE A THINK* THEN WHILE WE GUARD THE PLANET FROM...WHAT WAS IT WE'RE GUARDING IT FROM AGAIN?

OH, THAT'S RIGHT! NOTHING AT ALL! BECAUSE ONLY INSANE PEOPLE WANT TO GO TO EARTH!

BREACH IN 9A, SIR. HEPHAESTUS CLASS.
PROBABLY FAMILY OF ATTACK VICTIMS TRYING TO REUNITE WITH LOVED ONES.
CHANGE THEIR MINDS, ENSIGN.
UNIDENTIFIED CRAFT, YOU ARE TRAVELING IN A QUARANTINE ZONE. POWER DOWN IMMEDIATELY OR WE WILL ENGAGE, OVER?
GUYS, I DON'T THINK "OPERATION: BEREAVED LEMMINGS" IS WORKING FOR US!
ARM WEAPONS, MARSHAL.
ARE YOU OUT OF YOUR MIND?! NO WAY WE CAN TAKE THEM ON!
WE WON'T HAVE TO.
TARGET IS ARMING WEAPONS, COMMANDER...
SIGH
LET THEM GO.
SEE?
WHY WASTE THE AMMO...

"...WHEN WE'RE ALREADY DEAD."
SOMEWHERE ON EARTH
NO LOTTERY NO LIFE!
LET THEM GO!
BETTER THEM THAN US!
SO MANY THIS TIME.
HOW LONG CAN WE SUSTAIN THIS, VAGER?
AS WE'VE DISCUSSED, THE NEED GROWS WITH EVERY SHIPMENT.
THREE MONTHS BEFORE POPULATION COLLAPSE BASED ON CURRENT PROJECTIONS.
REMIND DR. ARGUS OF OUR TIMELINE. I WANT A FULL REPORT IN--
KESTREL!
PAF!
THESE MEN ARE SAYING THAT GIAN HAS BEEN SELECTED!
TELL THEM THEY'VE MADE A MISTAKE!

I WILL NOT DO THAT, GIAN.
I'M SORRY.
WHAT--?! YOU... YOU WOULD CONDEMN MY SON...YOUR OWN BLOOD TO--?!
IF I WERE TO EXEMPT GIAN, ANOTHER WOULD HAVE TO TAKE HIS PLACE. SOMEONE JUST AS DESERVING OF BEING SPARED.
THE TRUST OUR PEOPLE HAVE IN MY LEADERSHIP IS THE ONLY THING HOLDING US TOGETHER. I WON'T VIOLATE IT...
...EVEN FOR FAMILY.
STOP!
NO, PLEASE--!

THEN YOU'LL SEND ME INSTEAD.
PAPA, YOU CAN'T...!
THAT IS YOUR CHOICE.

SSSHHH...BE STRONG NOW, HIJO. KESTREL WILL TAKE CARE OF YOU. DO WHAT SHE SAYS.

I *WILL* SAVE US, MERO.
I WONDER, KES...

WHO'S GOING TO SAVE US...

...FROM YOU?

"GREETINGS AND SALUTATIONS, LIGHTNING BUGS!"
WELCOME BACK TO "THIS AIN'T YOUR DADDY'S WEATHER SHOW!" REDD BAY'S COOLEST WEATHER FORECAST!
WHY'S THE SHOW SO COOL, YOU ASK? BECAUSE WE'RE SO CRAZY! HOW CRAZY? GOOD QUESTION! LET'S JUST SAY...
...REAL CRAZY.
S M T W TH F S SOL
:517

ROYD FILBERT?! THEY REPLACED ME WITH ROYD FILBERT?!
THAT GUY'S A TOTAL SQUARE!
7-DAY FORCAST

ZAP! ZAP!
ZAP!
ZAP!
PAF
ZAP!
ZAP! ZAP!
PAF
NICE HAIRCUT, ROYD!

HEY, LIGHT BRITE, ARE YOU SEEING THIS?

ROYO FILBERT
HE'S DOING IT ALL WRONG!
HA HA HA HA HA HA HA HA HA
YOU LOSE AGAIN!!!
SNAP!
KRAK
FIFTEEN YEARS AGO, MIDAS MATERIALS SENT A DIGGER CREW TO MINE THE ICE ON CALLISTO.
THEY WERE LOOKING FOR TITANIUM. THEY FOUND SOMETHING ELSE.
"OR RATHER, IT FOUND US.

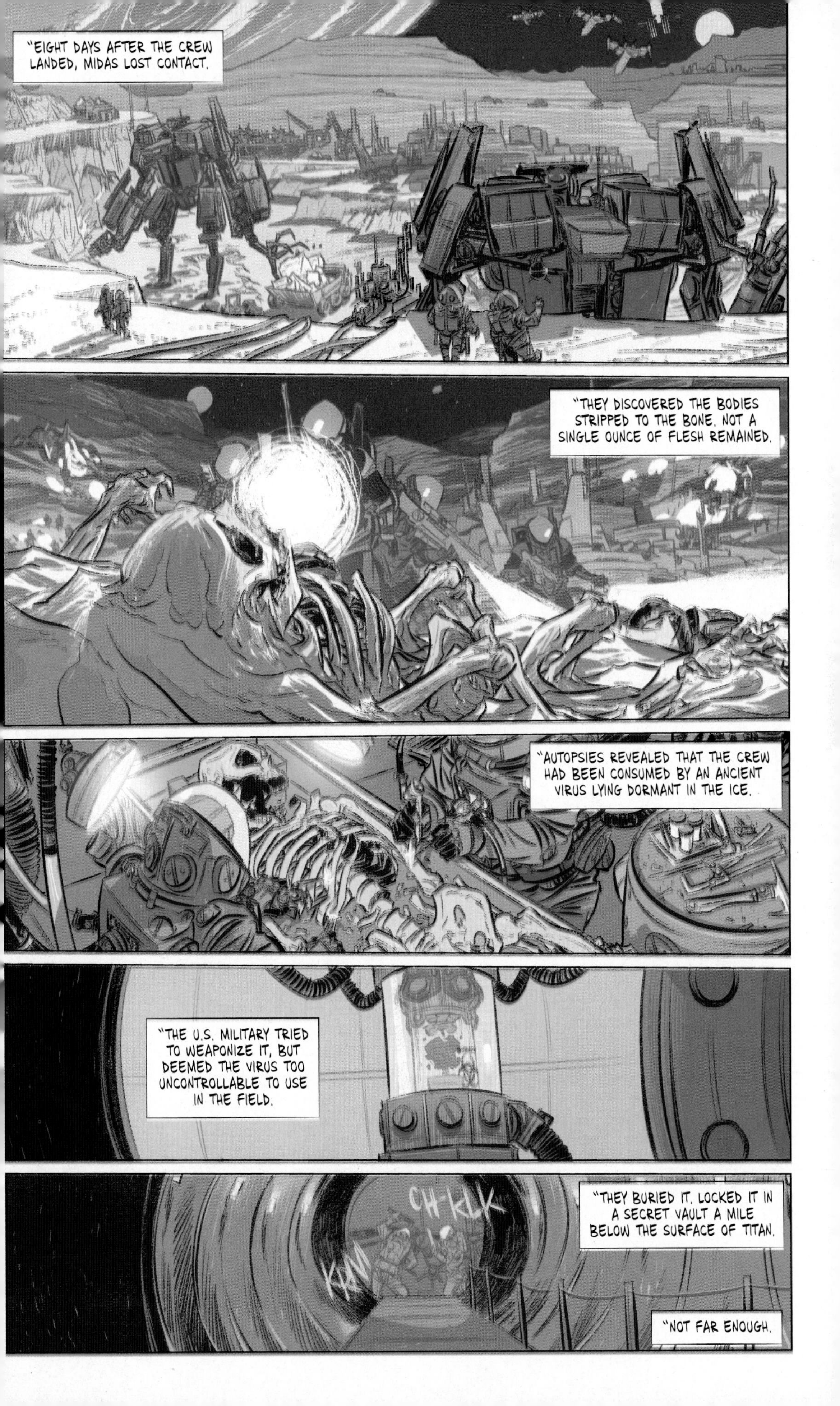
"EIGHT DAYS AFTER THE CREW LANDED, MIDAS LOST CONTACT.
"THEY DISCOVERED THE BODIES STRIPPED TO THE BONE. NOT A SINGLE OUNCE OF FLESH REMAINED.
"AUTOPSIES REVEALED THAT THE CREW HAD BEEN CONSUMED BY AN ANCIENT VIRUS LYING DORMANT IN THE ICE.
"THE U.S. MILITARY TRIED TO WEAPONIZE IT, BUT DEEMED THE VIRUS TOO UNCONTROLLABLE TO USE IN THE FIELD.
"THEY BURIED IT. LOCKED IT IN A SECRET VAULT A MILE BELOW THE SURFACE OF TITAN.
CH-KLK
KRAM
"NOT FAR ENOUGH.

"A FORMER ORCA OPERATIVE NAMED *IAN BLACK* BROKE INTO THE VAULT AND DELIVERED THE VIRUS TO *JAZEN JENNER,* THE LEADER OF THE SWORD OF GOD.
"JENNER RELEASED IT INTO EARTH'S POPULATION ON MAY 23RD, 2763. SEVEN YEARS AGO.
"SO FAR IT'S KILLED OVER EIGHTEEN BILLION PEOPLE.
"ONLY A FEW OUTPOSTS OF HUMANITY REMAIN.
"NO HELP IS COMING FOR THEM, NO CURE HAS BEEN FOUND, AND THERE'S NO HOPE OF GETTING OFF-WORLD.
"THE SURVIVORS WILL LIVE OUT THEIR LIVES BATTLING THE VIRUS, AND EVENTUALLY THEY'LL DIE TOO."

WHY GO TO EARTH THEN?
AFTER THE ATTACK, A FRINGE SCIENTIST NAMED NYSETH REMOVED IAN BLACK'S MEMORY AND REPLACED IT WITH THAT OF CLUELESS LOCAL WEATHERMAN *NATHAN BRIGHT.*
SHE THEN STORED BLACK'S OLD IDENTITY ON A SPECIAL *HARD DRIVE.*
I HAVE REASON TO BELIEVE THAT NYSETH IS ON EARTH. FIND HER AND WE FIND THE HARD DRIVE. FIND THE HARD DRIVE AND WE FIND JENNER.
CHAK!
AND THE WEATHERMAN?
WE KEEP HIM ALIVE UNTIL WE CAN SWAP HIM BACK TO BLACK. NO SMALL TAS BUT I THINK HE CAN HANDLE HIMSELF.

BOOM
BOOM
BOOM
BOOM
BOOM
THERE YOU GO! POP IT, GIRL! NICE!

BOOM
CHAK!
HEY! LET'EM TWERK LET'EM LIVE, BABY!
BOO-
SHUT IT DOWN, NATHAN!

GOOD IDEA! HERE, I'LL JUST PUT IT BACK ON "SAD SACK" RADI--

--OOOOOOOOOOOH...

THWAP!

SKRIITCH!
Y'ALL AIN'T GOT BOOTIES TO SHAKE. YOU KNOW THAT, RIGHT?
SOUP'S ON!
YOU JUST GOT SAVED BY THE DINNER BELL, MARSHAL!
I DON'T THINK YOU CAN SHAME-EAT SPACE GRUEL.
I'LL MAKE IT WORK.

GASP!
UNCTUOUS SAVORY DELIGHTS!
WOW.
YOU CAN COOK?

FUNNY WHAT YOU PICK UP WHEN YOU'RE DOING HARD TIME.
VALUABLE LIFE SKILLS, APPARENTLY. YOU SHOULD BE THANKING ME.
FOR THE LIFE SKILLS OR FOR STABBING ME IN THE BACK?
LOOK, *UH*...SORRY, CHIEF, WHAT'S YOUR NAME AGAIN?
GARREN.
TAP TAP
SURE, LISTEN...

...I KNOW YOU'RE SUPER HOT AND WORK OUT SO MUCH YOU DON'T HAVE TIME TO DO FUN STUFF AND THAT'S...ALSO SUPER HOT BUT...YOU CAN DIAL BACK THE CHARM OFFENSIVE.
CROSS AND I HAVE A *PRE-TTY* SERIOUS THING GOING ON SO...YOU KNOW... FAIR WARNING.
I JUST DON'T WANT TO SEE YOU GET HURT.

HE ALWAYS LIKE THIS?
A HUNDRED PERCENT.
GONNA BE A LONG SUICIDE MISSION.

WHAT'S WITH THE SPREAD?

SORT OF A TRADITION WITH MY CREW. BIG MEAL BEFORE A BIG SCORE.

SMA

KRASSHH

TOOK ME A WHOLE DAY TO MAKE THAT RAMEN.
WHAT'S HER PROBLEM?
WHITE LIGHT'S STILL STEAMED 'BOUT CROSS WHOOPIN' HER ASS.
WHY DO THEY CALL HER THAT ANYWAY?
WHERE WE HEADED, CROSS?

NEW YORK.
NEW YORK WAS LOST YEARS AGO.
ACCORDING TO WETZEL, THERE'S STILL AN OUTPOST THERE.
AND... *UH...* *NOM NOM* HOW ARE WE SUPPOSED TO GET OFF EARTH ONCE WE GET THE HARD DRIVE?

I'M WORKING ON IT.

GREAT! NOW ALL WE HAVE TO DO IS *NOT DIE* SO YOU CAN *KILL ME!*
UH... CROSS... WHERE ARE YOU--?

GOT'EM ALL FOOLED, DON'T YOU?

A DANCIN' WEATHERMAN.
BUT YOU AND I KNOW BETTER, DON'T WE.

WHAT YOU ARE. IT'S IN YOUR BONES.
THAT'S WHY WHEN THIS IS OVER I'M GONNA CUT'EM OUT. LISTEN TO YOUR SCREAMS LIKE THE SWEETEST SYMPHONY.
BATHE MYSELF IN YOUR BLOOD.

THAT DAY'S COMIN', WEATHERMAN.
DON'T FORGET.
DON'T EVER FORGET.

"THE SOLAR COUNCIL CAN'T CONTINUE THERMAL DROPS WITHOUT YOUR VOTE, MADAM PRESIDENT."
THAT'S RIGHT, COUNCILMAN. AS LONG AS THERE ARE CIVILIANS FIGHTING FOR SURVIVAL ON EARTH'S SURFACE--
THEY CAN'T BATTLE THE CONTAGION FOREVER. THEY *WILL* SUCCUMB. AND BY OUR ESTIMATES, WELL BEFORE SURFACE TEMPERATURES RISE HIGH ENOUGH TO KILL THEM.
WHAK
THOSE ARE HUMAN BEINGS DOWN THERE, CYRUS. YOU SHOULD BE WORKING TO PREVENT THEIR DEATHS, NOT PROFITING FROM THEM.
LET'S NOT BE MELODRAMATIC. WE'RE JUST GETTING A HEAD START ON THE INEVITABLE. THE SOONER WE RE-CLAIM EARTH--
THE SOONER YOU CAN AUCTION OFF REBUILDING CONTRACTS AND THEN IT'S BUSINESS AS USUAL UNTIL THE NEXT APOCALYPSE.
YOU TELL THE LOBBYISTS THAT UNTIL WE FIND AN ALTERNATE SOLUTION, I'M GOING TO OPPOSE THERMAL DROP CONTINUANCE.
AND WE'LL FILE A MOTION OF NO CONFIDENCE.
IF YOU COULD, YOU WOULDN'T BE ASKING ME FOR MY VOTE.
WHO SAYS I'M ASKING?

YOUR ADMINISTRATION HAS FAILED TIME AND AGAIN TO APPREHEND THE SWORD OF GOD, WHO *CONTINUES* TO TERRORIZE THE PUBLIC AT LARGE.

I'M OFFERING YOU THE CHANCE TO GIVE HUMANITY A VICTORY.

SEE, MADAM PRESIDENT...

...YOU AREN'T THE ONLY ONE ON A MISSION OF MERCY.

PLUK

FILE YOUR MOTION, COUNCILMAN, AND I'LL FILE ONE OF MY OWN.

I'M SURE COUNCILMAN TROV WILL BE VERY INTERESTED TO LEARN ABOUT YOUR RECENT MEETINGS WITH HIS DAUGHTER.

HOW OLD IS SHE AGAIN?

SHE'S OF AGE.
BARELY.
IT WON'T STOP HIM.
NO...

...BUT IT'LL BUY US SOME TIME.

TIME TO GO, NATHAN...
...NNNNHHH...
MAYBE I SHOULD JUST STAY HERE.

WHERE YOU'LL BE DOING *WHAT* EXACTLY?
COWERING.
IT'S ONE OF MY CORE COMPETENCIES.

YOU AREN'T LEAVING MY SIDE UNTIL THIS IS DONE. C'MON, GET UP.
YOU GET UP.
LOOK, I KNOW YOU'RE SCARED...

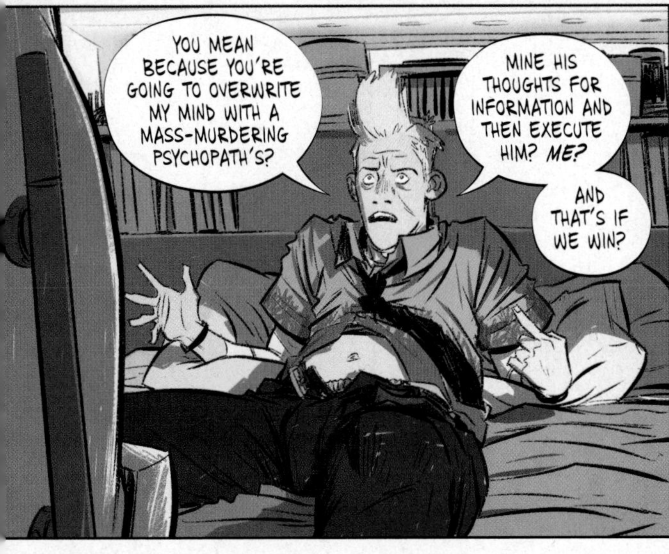
YOU MEAN BECAUSE YOU'RE GOING TO OVERWRITE MY MIND WITH A MASS-MURDERING PSYCHOPATH'S?
MINE HIS THOUGHTS FOR INFORMATION AND THEN EXECUTE HIM? *ME?*
AND THAT'S IF WE WIN?

ALSO THE MARSHAL SAYS HE'S GOING TO CUT MY BONES OUT.

NO ONE'S GOING TO CUT YOUR BONES OUT. LISTEN TO ME...
...EVERY SECOND THAT PASSES, JENNER GETS CLOSER TO LAUNCHING A SECOND ATTACK.
WE HAVE A CHANCE TO STOP THAT FROM HAPPENING. BUT WE CAN'T DO IT WITHOUT YOU.

I NEED YOU...*WE* NEED YOU...TO FIND THE STRENGTH TO HELP US. BECAUSE IF YOU DON'T, BILLIONS MORE INNOCENT PEOPLE ARE GOING TO DIE.
AND THAT, YOU WON'T BE ABLE TO BLAME ON IAN BLACK.

YOU SAY YOU'RE A DIFFERENT MAN, NATHAN.

PROVE IT.

"WHAT'S WITH THE SUITS? THE AIR'S BREATHABLE, RIGHT?"
"THE VIRUS CAN CONSUME A HUMAN FORM IN SECONDS. THE SUITS KEEP IT FROM COMING IN CONTACT WITH OUR SKIN."
LOOK OUT FOR FAST-MOVING, CLOUD-LIKE MISTS. THOSE ARE VIRAL COLLECTIVES.
SO...CROSS, DO YOU DO THIS KIND OF STUFF ALL THE TIME? LIKE ARE YOU MARRIED TO YOUR JOB OR DO YOU HAVE A NORMAL LIFE SOMEWHERE?
NORMAL IS FOR BETAS.
PSSH-- RIIIIIGHT?
NATHAN...
INSIDE VOICE. GOT IT.
MY...

...BAD.

C'MON.

WE HAVE TO KEEP--
NO.
HE NEEDS TO SEE THIS.

THIS ISN'T GOING TO GET EASIER, IS IT?

SMAK
YEAH, BUT LOOK ON THE BRIGHT SIDE.

THEY'RE *DEAD*.

"THEY AIN'T MAD ATCHA ANYMORE."

TO BE CONTINUED!...
GASP!
NO!

PICKLES!
WE HAVE TO GO BACK!
MUH?
YES, RIGHT NOW!
EARTH.
NEW YORK CITY RUINS.

MUH!
MUH! MUH!
LET'S GO, YOU BIG BABY!
FINE. I'LL DO IT MYSELF.
WHUMP

UNH!
EH!

NNN...
GH!

HUFF

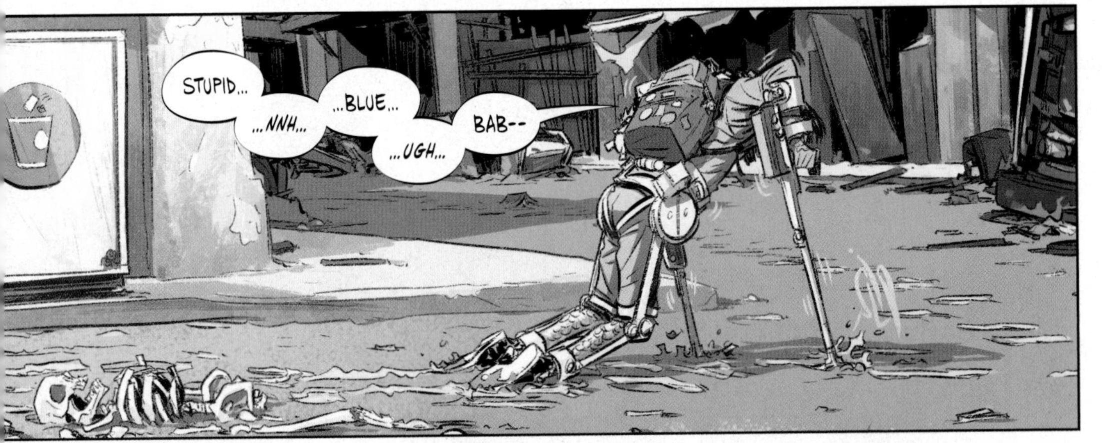
STUPID...
...NNH...
...BLUE...
...UGH...
BAB--

--EEEEEE!

YAY!
GRUMBLE
GRUMBLE

ELSEWHERE.
ALRIGHT, FRIEND. THAT TIME AGAIN.
YOU KNOW THE DRILL.

LET'S NOT MAKE THIS ANY HARDER THAN IT HAS TO BE.
EHK?!

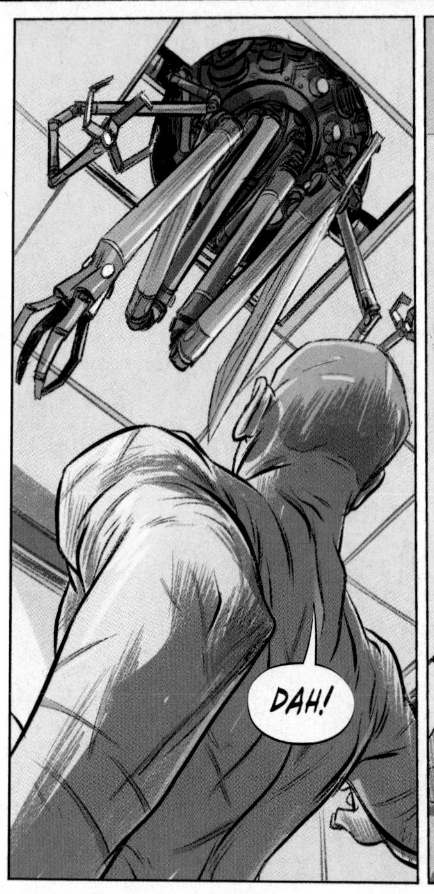
DAH!

APOLOGIES.
I KNOW THIS HURTS.

THAT WHAT THEY CALL AN EXACT SCIENCE?

AH, KESTREL. I WAS HOPING YOU WOULD NEEDLESSLY INTERRUPT ME.
YOU COULD HAVE PUT HIM UNDER FIRST.
AND YOU COULD HAVE KNOCKED. NOW YOU'VE CAUGHT MUM AND DAD IN THE SACK. HOW *CONFUSED* YOU MUST BE.

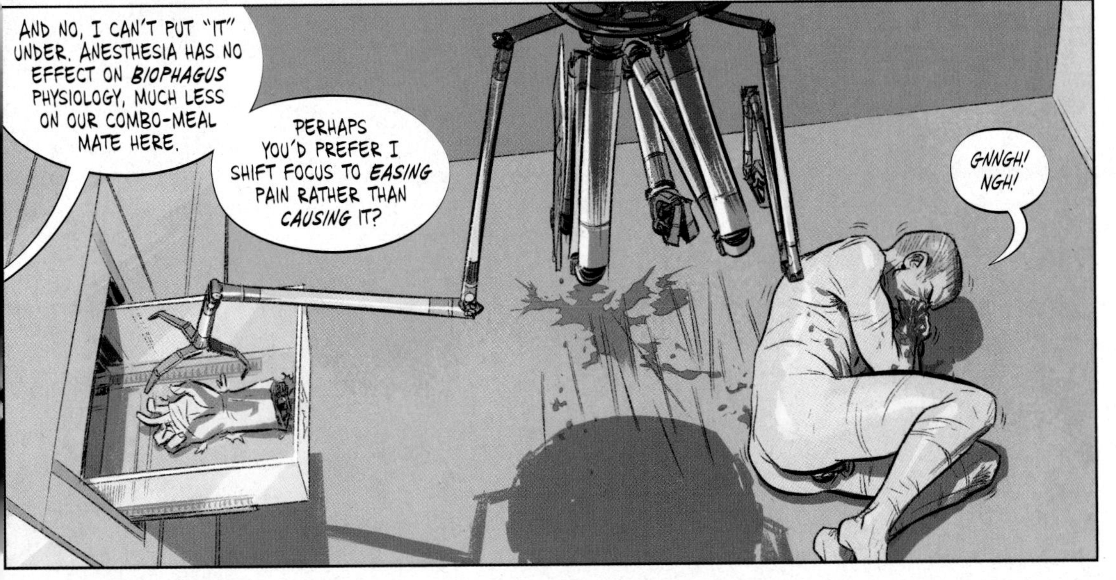
AND NO, I CAN'T PUT "IT" UNDER. ANESTHESIA HAS NO EFFECT ON *BIOPHAGUS* PHYSIOLOGY, MUCH LESS ON OUR COMBO-MEAL MATE HERE.
PERHAPS YOU'D PREFER I SHIFT FOCUS TO *EASING* PAIN RATHER THAN *CAUSING* IT?
GNNGH! NGH!

THE TRANSPORTS ARE FUELED AND READY TO DEPART. WHERE DO WE STAND, DR. ARGUS?
VREEE
WE'LL NEED ANOTHER MONTH. MAYBE LONGER. AND MORE CONTROL SPECIMENS.
I'LL SEND A DROP.
ANYTHING ELSE?

DOCTOR, I'VE BATTLED MY WHOLE LIFE TO KEEP OUR PEOPLE SAFE.
I ALWAYS THOUGHT I'D DIE FOR THEM.

NOW I SEND THEM TO DIE FOR ME.

I JUST NEED TO KNOW THAT THIS ISN'T ALL FOR NOTHING.
CAN YOU DO WHAT YOU SAY YOU CAN DO?
WITH ENOUGH TIME...WITH NYSETH'S HELP...
SPLAT!

CRUNCH
CRUNCH
YES.
I BELIEVE WE CAN.
CRUNCH!

KEEP ME INFORMED.

WHISSSSH
TEK
WHOOOOOSH

NEW YORK CITY RUINS.

OH, BLACK RAIN.
THAT'S A GOOD SIGN.
SOME SURVIVORS TRIED TO USE NUKES TO KILL THE VIRUS.
NATHAN, PERHAPS YOU'D LIKE TO EDUCATE US ON THE CLIMATE EFFECTS OF NUCLEAR FALLOUT?
WELL DO YOU HAVE AN ATMOSPHERIC SCIENCES DEGREE FROM THE UNIVERSITY OF NEW TEXAS (GO SALT MINERS)? BECAUSE IF YOU DON'T--
AHEM!
DAY IS FUN DAY

GASP! DINOSAUR PETTING ZOO!
PET -A- DINOSAUR
GENETIC APPROXIMATIONS. MOST LIKELY CONSUMED BY THE VIRUS.
DO WE KNOW WHAT WE'RE LOOKING FOR?
TECHNICALLY...?
EXISTENTIALLY.
NO. BUT I HAVE A FEELING WE'LL KNOW IT WHEN WE--
HELP ME!

HEEELLLP MEEE...

CAREFUL.
GRRRT
TAK
RBBBLL

EASY, NOW. I GOT YOU.
YOU'RE OKAY.

WHAT HAPPENED HERE?
ARE THERE OTHERS LIKE YOU?
OTHER SURVIVORS?

HELP ME.

WHAT IN--?

GET BACK!

GARREN?!
I'LL BE OKAY...
I DON'T KNOW WHAT'S HAPPENING. INTEL DIDN'T SAY ANYTHING ABOUT--

THEY FORGOT TO MENTION THE *MANTIS-LADY*?!
GOTTA GET 'IM BACK TO THE *DISCO QUEEN*.
THE HELL HAVE YOU GOTTEN US INTO?!

OH, MAN. I HAD A DREAM LIKE THIS ONCE. ONLY IN THE DREAM THE NAKED PEOPLE WERE HOTTIES.
AND FOR SOME REASON I HAD A DOG PENIS.
NATHAN...

RUN!

NOPE!
PAGES FROM THE AGE
ESTABLISHED 2237
NOPE!
NOPE!

ESTABLISHED 2237
BOR-ING!

SQUEEL!
YES!
MEGA NINJA BATTLE PRINCESS

OKAY, FUZZY FACE, LET'S--
WHAT IS IT?
GRRRRR RR

OH NO...

NATHAN, BEHIND YOU!

AAAAAAAAH!
BLAM
BLAM
THK

GET UP, NATHAN!
WHAT?! I--
TAKA TAKA TAKAH

GET UP!

FWOOM
BAM
BAM
TAKAKA
KOOM
BOOM
HANG ON! WE'RE ALMOST THERE!
GAININ'... ON US. NOT GONNA...HNG... MAKE IT...
TAKA
TAKAK
CLIK
KLAK
BLAM
TAKAKA
HEY! WHAT ARE YOU--?!
PAFF
CLIK
CAN'T SAVE EVERYONE, AMY.
CHAK
WHAT?!
MARSHAL!

NO!
BLAM
BLAM
BLAM
BLAM
BLAM
GARREN!
UNH!
FUCK YOU!
DON'T... FORGET ME...

AAGGHHH
BANG
BANG
THEY'RE CRAWLING ALL OVER THE SHIP!
BANG
BANG
BANG
BANG
CAN THEY GET IN?
OL' DISCO'S GOT A HARD BARK. DON'T SEE'EM BREACHIN' IT ANY TIME SOON.
BANG
BANG
BANG
BANG
BANG
BANG
YEAH?
BANG

HOW 'BOUT NOW?!

POK!
BOOM!
KLK
K-CHAK
SPUT
TSSSSS
VVVVREE
EEEE

CHA- CHAK

RAHHHH
KRAK
SWAP
ZURCH
ZWIP!

UM...WHAT JUST--?
IT'S A LOCALIZED MICRO SINGULARITY.
TOTALLY. WHAT'S THAT?
A BLACK HOLE BULLET. MILITARY GRADE MUNITIONS. QUESTION IS, WHO WOULD--?

HELLOOO-OOO!
YOU CAN COME OUT NOW!
PICKLES SAYS IT'S SAFE!
DISCO QUEEN

OPEN THE DOOR, MARSHAL.
I DON'T THINK THAT'S A--
OPEN IT.

WHO ARE YOU?
I'M PACE! THE BIG FUZZY IS PICKLES.
WHY ARE YOU HELPING US?

YOU'RE PEOPLE. REAL PEOPLE. LIKE ME!
WE'RE LOOKING FOR SOMEONE, PACE. ANOTHER REAL PERSON...DOING RESEARCH...

DO YOU KNOW WHERE WE CAN FIND THIS WOMAN?

SOON.
C'MON, SLOW POKES!
ALMOST THERE!

HEY, CROSS... UH...
I KNOW I SLOWED US DOWN BACK THERE. I WISH I WAS BETTER AT...
I WAS SCARED. I DON'T KNOW...FROZEN.

WHITE LIGHT SAID--
I KNOW WHAT SHE SAID! THANKS!

WELL...
...AT LEAST WE'RE ON THE RIGHT TRACK, HUH? SNIPER-GIRL AND FUZZ ALDRIN SEEM TO KNOW WHERE THEY'RE GOIN' SO...

...MAYBE WE'LL CATCH A BREAK.

"GOD KNOWS...
TA-DAAAH!
"...WE COULD USE A WIN."

BRUTAL
NOODLES
ENJOY
HAVE A BRUTAL DAY

3

WELP! LOOKS LIKE WE CAN'T WIPE MY MIND AND REPLACE IT WITH A PSYCHO'S. *SUCKS!*
PLAN B PITCH: LET'S G.T.F.O., BUILD OUR OWN ICE CREAM SUNDAES, AND HAVE A SUMO-SUIT DANCE PARTY.
WHAT DO YOU THINK?
I THINK YOU'RE ALREADY A PSYCHO.
YOU ARE.

DOO-DUM-DEE-DUM-DUM-DUM

HEY, BUD!
SUN'S OUT!

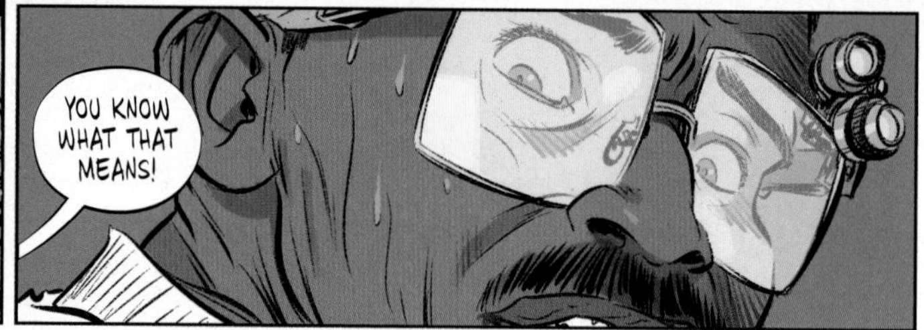
YOU KNOW WHAT THAT MEANS!

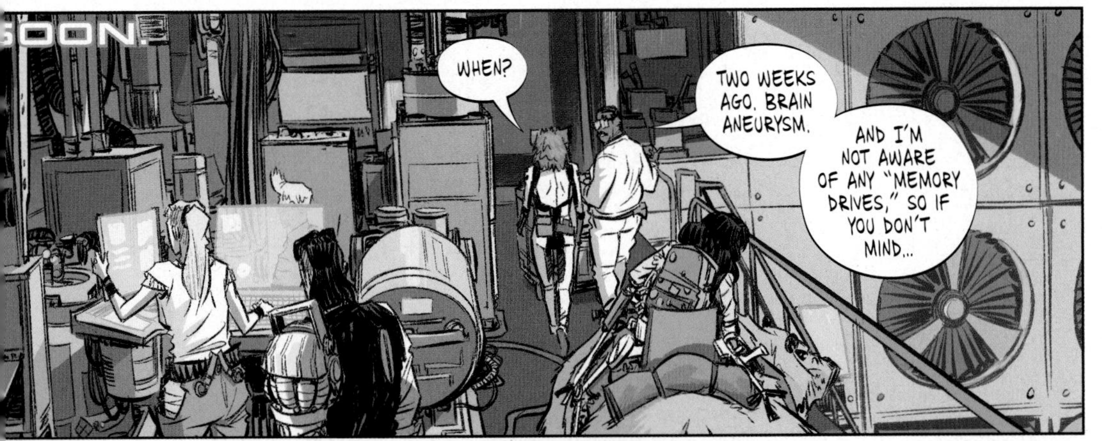
WHEN?
TWO WEEKS AGO. BRAIN ANEURYSM.
AND I'M NOT AWARE OF ANY "MEMORY DRIVES," SO IF YOU DON'T MIND...

I UNDERSTAND NYSETH WAS TRYING TO FIND A CURE FOR THE VIRUS.
NOT A CURE. A *WEAPON.* AND *BIOPHAGUS PROTEUS* ISN'T A VIRUS. IT'S A SINGLE-CELL ORGANISM THAT FLASH-FEEDS ON ANIMAL DNA. MORE LIKE A PROTOZOAN.
(NOT THAT ANYONE GIVES A SHIT ABOUT DETAILS ANYMORE.)

ON OUR WAY HERE WE WERE ATTACKED BY... PEOPLE...ANIMALS... COMING OUT OF THE MISTS.
YES, OVER TIME BIOPHAGUS INDIVIDUALS HAVE LEARNED TO COMBINE THEMSELVES INTO COMPLEX FORMS, TO MIMIC DNA THEY'VE CONSUMED.
WHEREAS BEFORE THEY SIMPLY APPEARED AS "MIST," THEY CAN NOW SHIFT INTO ANY ANIMAL THEY'VE TASTED. OR AMALGAMATIONS THEREOF.
HELPS THEM LURE PREY, OPEN DOORS, ETC... WE CALL THOSE FORMS "CONSTRUCTS." VERY DANGEROUS, THOSE.

EXCUSE ME...PLEASE DON'T TOUCH THAT.
IT'S OKAY. I'M A SCIENTIST TOO SO...
YES, A *WEATHERMAN,* I UNDERSTAND. IF YOU'RE LOOKING FOR THE MILK AND COOKIES THEY'RE OVER--

MILK AND COOKIES?!

OH, YOU WERE BEING MEAN.

TELL ME ABOUT THIS WEAPON.
EACH BIOPHAGE CONTAINS A SHORT-RANGE PHEROMONE CALLED *"NEUROPRESSIN"* THAT ENABLES THE ORGANISM TO COMMUNICATE WITH ITSELF TELEPATHICALLY. LIKE A HIVE MIND.

AFTER IT WAS DISCOVERED, MILITARY SCIENTISTS BEGAN TO EXPERIMENT WITH NEUROPRESSIN IN HUMANS. HENCE THE HANDFUL OF PSYCHICS RUNNING 'ROUND.
OUR BREAKTHROUGH OCCURRED WHEN WE REALIZED WE COULD USE THEIR CONNECTION TO OUR ADVANTAGE.

POISON THE WELL.
INDEED. NYSETH AND I WERE BUILDING A KIND OF *GENE BOMB* THAT, ONCE CONSUMED, WOULD SPREAD A KILL CO VIA THE NEUROPRESSIN PHEROMONE, ULTIMATEL TRIGGERING CELL DEAT SPECIES-WIDE.

THIS... GENE BOMB. WHERE IS--?

AH!

THAT MAN IS THE--?
USED TO BE OUR LAB ASSISTANT, REGI. BUT NO, NOT A MAN. NOT ANYMORE. A *HYBRID*. PART BIOPHAGE, PART HUMAN.
WHEN OUR WORK IS DONE, IT WILL BE GIVEN OVER TO THE CONSTRUCTS AND THE KILL CODE IN HIS GENES WILL DESTROY THEM.

NOT...A MAN...
IT CAN... TALK?
THAT IS OUR HOPE.
CONSTRUCTS CAN'T UNDERSTAND SPEECH BUT THEY CAN MIMIC IT. LIKE A PARROT.

NOTHIN' HERE.
THERE HAS TO BE SOMEWHERE ELSE. SOMEWHERE NYSETH MIGHT HAVE STORED HER OLD RESEARCH.
NOTHING COMES TO--

WAIT...SYNGEN STATION.

THE LAB WE WERE ASSIGNED TO WHEN MIRIAM FIRST CAME TO EARTH.
IT'S POSSIBLE THE IAN BLACK MEMORY DRIVE IS THERE BUT... YOU'D NEED A KEY...
WE'LL MANAGE. WHERE'S THE LAB?

YOU DON'T UNDERSTAND. SYNGEN WAS ONE OF THE MOST HIGHLY PROTECTED FACILITIES IN THE WORLD. THE CENTER OF BIOPHAGUS RESEARCH.
ALL TECHNICIANS ENTERING THE LAB HAD TO BE SCANNED AND THEIR DNA PROFILES EXACTLY MATCHED TO ONES ON FILE. YOU CAN'T JUST WALK IN AND--
NOPE.
SYN GEN

BUT YOU CAN.

WHOA, WHOA, WHOA...YOU HEARD WHAT HE SAID! WHAT ABOUT--?
MOVE, NATHAN.
I SYMPATHIZE WITH YOUR PLIGHT, BUT I WILL NOT LEAVE THIS LAB. WE'VE SACRIFICED TOO MUCH AND I'M TOO CLOSE.

DON'T LECTURE ME ABOUT SACRIFICE!
CROSS...HE COULD END THE VIR--PROTO--HE COULD END IT. FOR GOOD. WE HAVE TO LET HIM TRY!
WHAT IF HE CAN'T DO IT, NATHAN?! WE DON'T HAVE TIME!
YOU KEEP SAYING THAT! IT'S NOT LIKE JENNER HAS ANOTHER--
TEK
ALARM
THERE WERE TWO SAMPLES. JENNER STILL HAS THE OTHER.
WHAT?!
WHY DIDN'T YOU TELL ME?
YOU MEAN LIKE THE LAST TIME I GAVE YOU CLASSIFIED INFORMATION?
WE'RE ALL GONNA DIE!

IF WE DON'T FIND IAN BLACK'S MEMORY DRIVE AND STOP THE SWORD OF GOD THERE MIGHT NOT BE PEOPLE LEFT. I'M NOT WILLING TO TAKE THAT CHANCE.
THAT'S FAIR.

ARE YOU?

PLEASE! YOU DON'T UNDERSTAND WHAT YOU'RE DOING! WHAT WE'VE HAD TO DO TO SURVIVE!

WHAT IS IT?

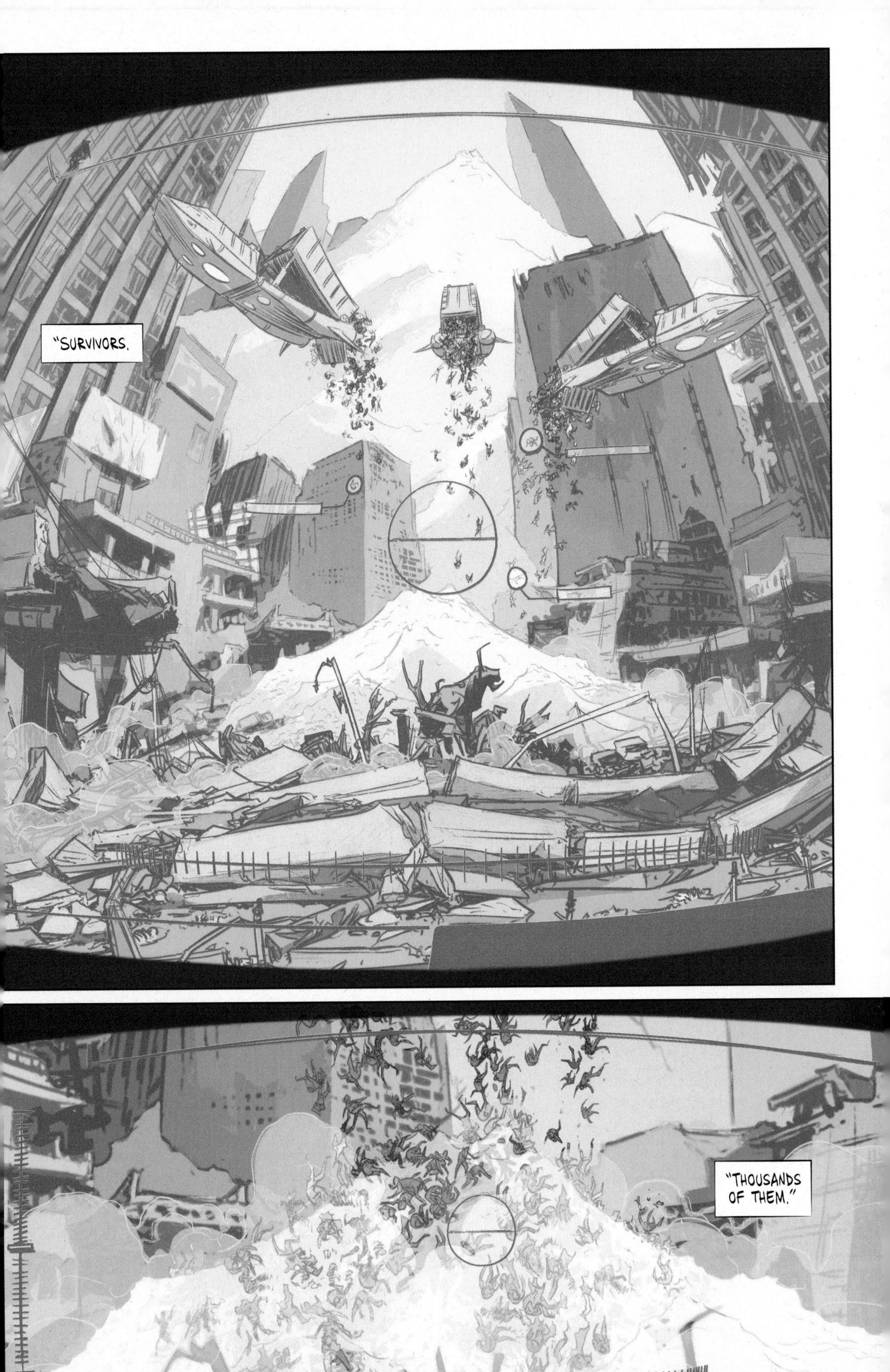
"SURVIVORS.
"THOUSANDS OF THEM."

"THE VIRUS...
"JESUS... YOU'RE--"

FEEDING IT.

BIOPHAGUS KNOWS WHERE WE ARE. BY COMING TO IT, WE CONTROL WHO DIES, HOW MANY, AND WHEN.
IT'S HOW WE'VE MANAGED TO BUY TIME.

IF YOU TAKE ME WITH YOU... ALL THOSE PEOPLE AND COUNTLESS MORE...
...WILL HAVE DIED FOR NOTHING.

CROSS, WE DON'T KNOW IF IAN'S MEMORY DRIVE STILL EXISTS.
OR IF THE INFO YOU NEED IS EVEN ON IT.

WHAT IF SOMETHING HAPPENS TO HIM?

HE COMES WITH US.
PACE, YOU WANNA COME TOO?
WOO-HOO! ADVENTURE TIME!
SKRATCH
SKRITCH
TUK
TUK

WE CAN SAVE THESE PEOPLE, CROSS.
NO, NATHAN...

...YOU CAN'T.

MARSHAL?
WE AIN'T ALONE.

I DON'T KNOW WHERE YOU CAME FROM...
...BUT I'M GLAD YOU'RE HERE.

WE COULD USE A FEW MORE WARM BODIES.

WHO ARE YOU?
WHY HAVE YOU STOLEN FROM US?
SNAP
I'D CLOSE MY EYES I WAS YOU.
WHAT?! WHY?!
CHAK
UNH!
AH!

HURK
TZAK

ELSEWHERE.
INTELLIGENCE SUGGESTS THAT ONE OF COMMANDER JENNER'S INNER CIRCLE--CODENAME "DJINN"--IS PLANNING TO BOMB A CIVILIAN POPULATION IN XANTHE.
SO BRING HER IN. WHAT ARE YOU WAITING FOR?

BURGA 2770
IT'S NOT THAT SIMPLE, MADAM PRESIDENT. WE'VE BEEN DOWN THIS ROAD BEFORE.

DJINN SWORD OF GOD
JENNER SWORD OF GOD
IF JENNER KNOWS WE HAVE HIS OPERATIVE, HE'LL CHANGE HIS PLANS. WE NEED TO ACQUIRE THE TARGET WITHOUT TIPPING OUR HAND.
OUR RECOMMENDATION IS THAT YOU ALLOW US TO TAKE DJINN INTO CUSTODY THEN EXECUTE THE REST OF HER PLOT.
JENNER WILL BELIEVE DJINN DIED IN THE ATTACK.
DOWN WITH BURGA
NO BURGA

YOU WANT TO BLOW UP OUR OWN PEOPLE?!
YOU CANNOT BE SERIOUS, DIRECTOR ZANE. FITCH WOULD NEVER HAVE SUGGESTED--
MY PREDECESSOR FAILED.
BUG OFF BURGA
TRUTH NOW
WE NEED TO START THINKING OUTSIDE THE BOX.

MADAM PRESIDENT...?
LOCK HER UP
VOTE BURGA

WE NEED AN ANSWER.

WHAT ARE YOUR ORDERS?
VOTE BURGA OUT!
THE ATTACK IS A HOAX!!!
BELIEVE IN BURGA
VOTE HER OUT!
JUSTICE NOW!
BURGA 2770!

"PARTYIN' WITH THE COOL KIDS, HUH?"

POK
POK
TIGHT.
THEY FASCINATE ME.

SCRATCH
SCRATCH
THOSE TWO HAVE WANDERED THE AREA FOR YEARS NOW. STRAY ANIMALS LIVING OFF THE LAND AND WHATEVER THEY CAN SALVAGE.

WHOA! HOLY CRAP!

IT'S OKAY!
WE'RE SAFE. FAR MORE SO THAN WE WOULD BE WITHOUT THEM.
DAMAGED?
"PICKLES" IS A CONSTRUCT BUT NOT LIKE THE OTHERS. DAMAGED BY RADIATION, WE SUSPECT.
THINK OF IT AS MENTALLY HANDICAPPED. HEALTHY BIOPHAGUS INDIVIDUALS TRY TO DESTROY IT ON SIGHT, SEEING PICKLES AS A FLAWED VERSION OF THEMSELVES.
I KNOW HOW *THAT* FEELS.
SOMEHOW PICKLES IS CONNECTED TO PACE WHO IT SEES AS A PRIMARY SOURCE OF FOOD.
IN EXCHANGE THE CONSTRUCT ACTS AS TRANSPORTATION AND PROTECTION, COMPENSATING FOR HER PHYSICAL HANDICAP.

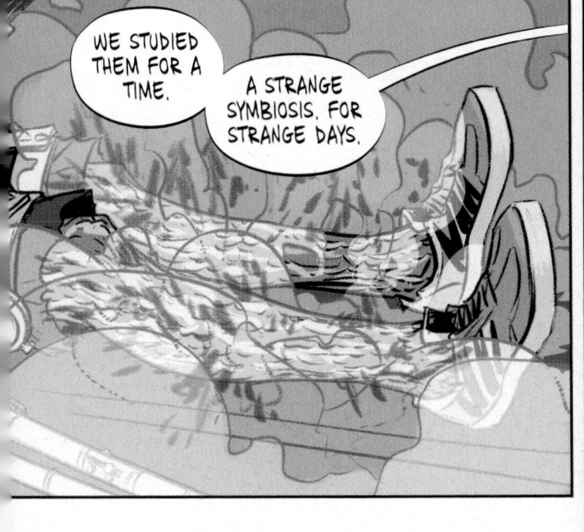
WE STUDIED THEM FOR A TIME.
A STRANGE SYMBIOSIS. FOR STRANGE DAYS.

I'D CALL THEM HARMLESS BUT...
...HERE I SIT.

YOU'RE ALL MAKING A BIG MISTAKE.
YEAH, WELL... WOULDN'T BE THE FIRST TIME. APPARENTLY I'M THE ONE THAT RELEASED THE VIRUS IN THE FIRST PLACE. OR AT LEAST GAVE IT TO THE GUY THAT DID.

YOU'RE IAN BLACK?
AFTER HE WIPED HIS MIND, YEAH. THAT'S WHAT THEY SAY, ANYWAY.
WHY ARE YOU TELLING ME THIS?

I DON'T KNOW.
I MEAN IT'S CRAZY, RIGHT? WITHOUT THE MEMORIES, I'M A COMPLETELY DIFFERENT GUY.

IS THAT WHY YOU SAT WITH ME? YOU THINK BECAUSE I'M A SCIENTIST I'LL BE ABLE TO LOOK *PAST* WHAT YOU *DID?*
TELL YOU YOU'RE *WORTH SOMETHING?*
YOU'RE *NOT.* SCIENTIFICALLY SPEAKING, THE CHEMISTRY THAT MOTIVATED YOUR ACTIONS IS STILL THERE.

ALL IT TAKES IS THE RIGHT SET OF CIRCUMSTANCES FOR YOU TO MAKE THE SAME CHOICES. FEEL BETTER?
NOW IF YOU'LL EXCUSE ME.

DOCTOR...
...WHAT HAPPENED TO NYSETH?

"MIRIAM WAS SELECTED IN THE LOTTERY. BUT BECAUSE OF OUR WORK SHE WAS EXEMPTED.
"A MOB FORMED OUTSIDE THE LAB. ANGRY THAT WE WERE BEING SPARED FOR A CURE THEY THOUGHT WOULD NEVER COME.
TSHHHH

E THOUGHT E COULD SON WITH CROWD.
"SHE WAS WRONG.
ONLY TIME I'VE VER KNOWN HER TO BE."

HER LAST MOMENTS WERE SPENT MAKING SURE I HAD WHAT I NEEDED TO CONTINUE TO PROTECT THE PEOPLE THAT TOOK HER LIFE.
WHY?

SHE WAS WORTH SOMETHING.

PAF
TEK

C'MON, C'MON...

BINGO.

FIND WHAT YOU'RE LOOKIN' FOR?
YOU SHOULD'VE TOLD ME.

YOUR TATTOO.
YOU WERE AN *ORCA*.

DID YOU KNOW HIM?
BLACK AND I SERVED TOGETHER. THEN WE WERE PARTNERS ON VENUS. BOUNTIES MOSTLY. 'FORE HE JOINED UP WITH JENNER'S CREW.
YOU WERE FRIENDS.
SHFFF
SHUT

"WE MADE MONEY."

WE MADE MORE OF IT TOGETHER.
WHY'D HE JOIN UP WITH JENNER?
NOT MY CONCERN.
ALL I KNOW IS HE WORE DOWN.

STARTED MAKIN' BAD DECISIONS.
AN' ON ACCOUNT OF HIS WEAKNESS...
POP!

...PEOPLE DIED.

24 HOURS AGO.
GREAT! JUST TORM OFF FROM HE TABLE WHEN NGS AREN'T GOING OUR WAY! WHAT XACTLY IS YOUR PROB--
SHFF
--LEM?
WHAT'S MY PROBLEM?! I KNOW YOU, AMY! HOW LONG BEFORE THE OTHERS REALIZE YOU DON'T HAVE A PLAN TO GET OFF EARTH?!
I'LL FIGURE SOMETHING OUT!
YEAH? WELL IT'S YOU VERSUS THE MOST HIGHLY MOTIVATED MILITARY FORCE EVER ASSEMBLED. GOOD LUCK WITH THAT!
JESUS, GARREN, YOU'RE SO GODDAMN SELFISH!
OH, I'M SELFISH?!
YOU KNEW WHAT THE STAKES WERE BEFORE YOU SIGNED ON!
YEAH, I DID!
SO WHY DID YOU?! HUH?! WHY?!
BMP
I THOUGHT MAYBE YOU COULD USE ME.

DEET DEET
YOU HAVE RRIVED AT YOUR DESTINATION.

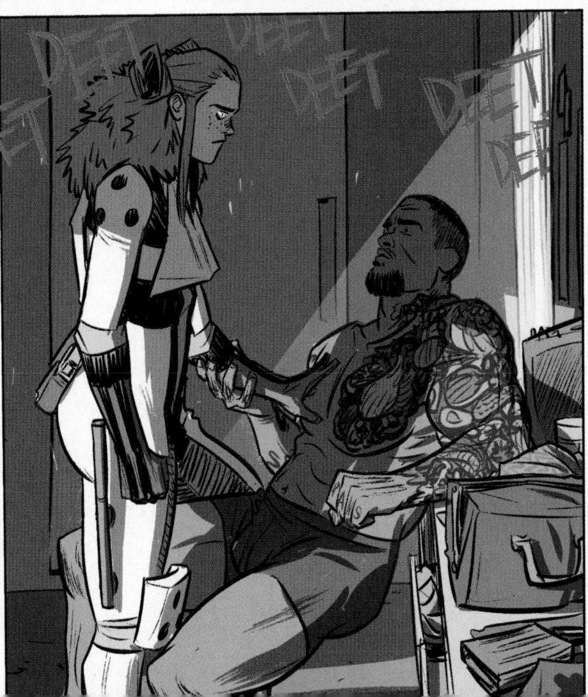
DEET DEET
DEET DEET

BRUTAL
NOODLES
ENJOY
HAVE A BRUTAL DAY

THE CANADIAN WILDERNESS.

FOCUS. LINE UP THE SIGHT WITH THE TARGET. AND SQUEEZE THE TRIGGER.

BAM BAM
NAILED IT.
MISSED AGAIN! HAHA!

ALL THIS FOCUS IS CRAMPING MY STYLE!
JUST GOTTA LET LOOSE!
FREEBALL IT!
NO, NATHAN, DON'T--!

BAM
BAM
BAM
SMAK
ONE...

...ON TARGET.

BOOM!
SUCK IT, FILBERT!
SNIFF SNIFF
SNIFF
THE SCARIES ARE COMING. WE SHOULD LEAVE.
GRRRRRRR
TWRR
SORRY, CROSS, YOU SHOULD PROLABY HANDLE THE GUN STUFF.
WHAT'S "PROLABY"?
IT'S LIKE A WALLABY ONLY MUCH MORE LIKELY.
I NEVER THOUGHT I'D SAY THIS TO AN INSANE PERSON BUT... PLEASE TAKE THE GUN.
ZZZAK
WHUMF
TINK TINK

SYNGEN STATION.
THE ARCTIC CIRCLE.

MARSHAL, YOU AND WHITE LIGHT STAY AND WATCH OUR BACKS. SOMETHING MIGHT HAVE FOLLOWED US OUT HERE.
CHAK
CHAK
CROSS, DID WE BRING SNACKS?
LOW BLOOD SUGAR CAN REALLY AFFECT DECISION-MAKING.

GENETIC IDENTITY CONFIRMED.

WELCOME BACK, DR. ARGUS.
K-CHUNK
CHAK
CHAK

THIS WAY.
NYSETH'S OFFICE IS ON THE LOWER LEVEL. IF IAN BLACK'S MEMORY IS HERE, THAT'S WHERE WE'LL FIND IT.

SERIOUSLY, DID WE?
SHUT *UP*, NATHAN.

WHOA.
YES, VERY IMPRESSIVE. LET'S JUST FIND IAN'S MEMORY DRIVE, GET OFF-WORLD, AND STOP THE SWORD OF GOD FROM KILLING WHAT'S LEFT OF HUMANITY.
YOU LEFT OUT THE PART WHERE YOU REPLACE MY MIND WITH IAN'S AND BASICALLY KILL ME.
DID I?

QUITE THE SETUP.
INDEED. A BIT DIFFICULT TO GET TO, BUT THE REMOTE LOCATION MEANT FEWER PRYING EYES. AND LESS COLLATERAL DAMAGE SHOULD SPECIMENS ESCAPE.
WHY ABANDON IT?

HEY, LOOK!
A JELLYFISH!
POKE
POKE
POKE

NO, YOU IDIOT!
GET AWAY FROM THE GLASS!

WHAT?

BOOM

KRAK
KRAK
KRAK

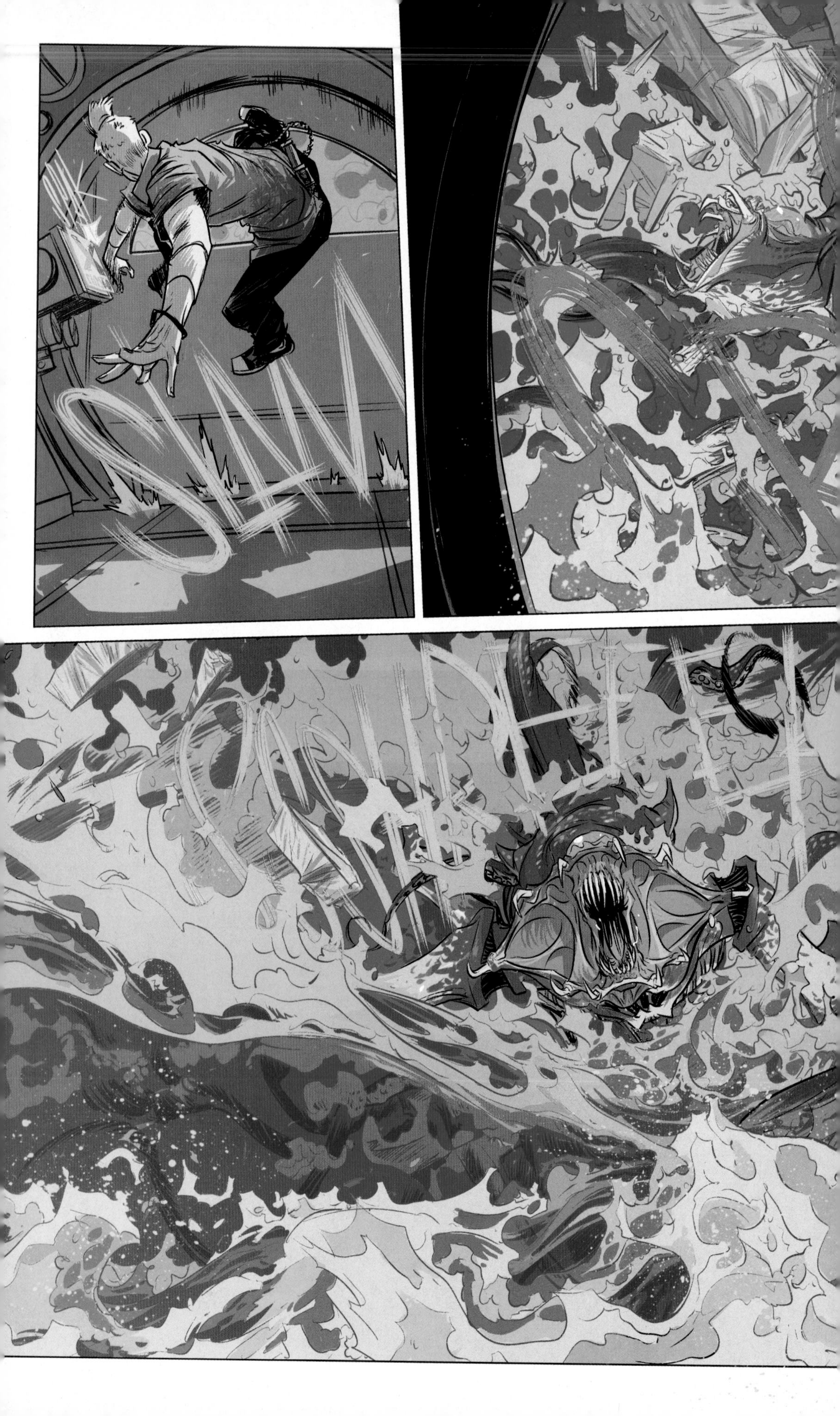

EMERGENCY

WHAM

CLOSED
THAT'S WHY.
NATHAN!

...CAN YOU HEAR ME?!
I'M HERE. I'M OKAY.
STAY WHERE YOU ARE.

NOPE!
I AM DEFINITELY NOT DOING THAT.
WE'LL CIRCLE AROUND. CAN YOU FIND SOMEWHERE SAFE TO HOLE UP?
PROLABY.
STOP SAYING THAT!

WHOOP! WHOOP!
HERE THEY COME!

CROSS...
=KSSH=-- GO AHEAD-- =KSSH=
WHATEVER YOU'RE DOIN'... DO IT FAST.
KLAKT

WE GOT INCOMING.

SHIT!
WHERE'S THE OFFICE?!
ALMOST THERE.

NATHAN, WHERE ARE YOU?
I FOUND THE MESS HALL! THEY HAVE FROZEN PIZZA! ≥NOM NOM NOM≤
MMF...IT'S TERRIBLE.
...
≥NOM NOM NOM≤

M. NYSETH
APPLIED NEUROGENETICS
STAY PUT.
WE WON'T BE--

--LONG.

TAKE HIM.
CLATCH

WHO ARE YOU?
HOW'D YOU GET IN WITHOUT--?

WHUMP!

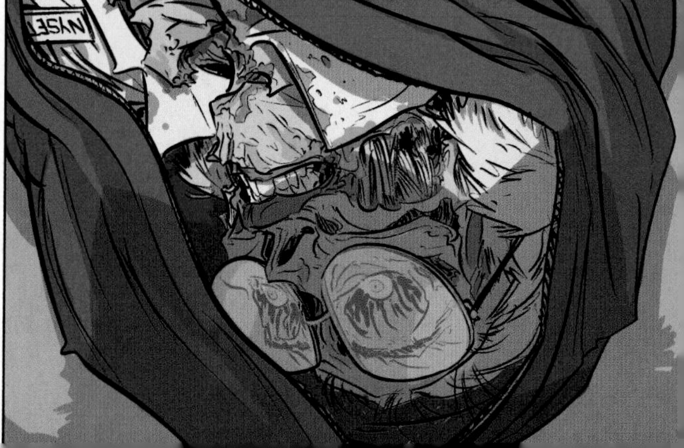

GAH!

OH NO! CROSS!
IT'S THE LOW BLOOD SUGAR... I BLAME MYSELF!
OKAY, NATHAN. BREATHE. *NOM NOM* THIS IS WHAT YOU TRAIN FOR.
LET'S DO--

--THIIIIIIS?!

WHAT WAS THAT?
FIND HIM.
THERE'S ANOTHER. A...WEATHERMAN.
LONG STORY.

OW.
IAN BLACK
WILLIAM PILGRIM

GO! GO! ON THE LEFT!
CLIK
CLIK

BMP
AIR VENT!

TAKAKAKAKAKAKAKAKAKAKAKAKA

LEAVE HIM. WE'RE OUTTA HERE.

GRAB WHAT YOU CAN.
ANYTHING THAT LOOKS IMPORTANT.
IAN BLACK

"TIME TO GO NOW, FUZZY FACE."

WHINE
WHINE
DON'T WORRY. I'LL COME BACK FOR YOU.
I PROMISE.

WHINE

DON'T HURT ME, PLEASE. I GIVE UP.

FIND THE OTHERS AND REPORT BACK.

NO...

WHUMPF

CHATTER
CHATTER

ABOUT TIME.

NO DISTRACTIONS.
NO HEROES.

JUST YOU AND ME.

Y-YOU'RE NOT SUPPOSED TO B-BE IN MY HEAD.
FUNNY, I WAS JUST THINKING THE SAME THING ABOUT YOU.

YOU KNOW WHY I'M HERE, DON'T YOU?
IT'S N-NOT MY FAULT.
WHOSE FAULT IS IT?

WHAT DO YOU SAY WE ASK THEM?

THAT'S WHY THEY'RE HERE, AFTER ALL.
JUSTICE IS ALL THAT'S LEFT NOW.
MAYBE IT'S TIME TO GIVE IT TO THEM.

SOON.
UNH...
WHERE ARE WE?
SKYBOROUGH.

AND I AM KESTREL ANDREA NOVARRO, FREELY ELECTED LEADER OF THIS OUTPOST.
WE'RE ABOVE NEW YORK... BUT...WHY--?
DIDN'T YOU SEE US?
YOU CHOSE NOT TO.
SKYBOROUGH WAS THE FIRST OF ITS KIND. A PRISON IN THE CLOUDS, PART OF A BEAUTIFICATION INITIATIVE.
A PLACE WHERE CRIMINALS WOULD BE OUT OF THE WAY. AND THANKS TO LIGHT-BENDING TECHNOLOGY, OUT OF SIGHT AS WELL.

SKYBOROUGH WAS SO SUCCESSFUL THAT IT WAS EXPANDED TO INCLUDE PUBLIC HOUSING. OVER TIME IT BECAME A FLOATING FAVELA OF THE POOR AND THE POWERLESS.
NOW IT IS ALL THAT REMAINS OF THE AMERICAN PEOPLE.

WE HAVE NO FIGHT WITH YOU. WE'RE SEARCHING FOR SOMETHING.
YES...A MEMORY. ARGUS BRIEFED ME ON YOUR OBJECTIVE.
THEN YOU KNOW HOW IMPORTANT IT IS. WE CAN STOP WHAT HAPPENED TO YOU FROM HAPPENING AGAIN.

LOOK DOWN.
WHAT DO YOU SEE?

"FURNACES.
"MASSIVE OVENS THE SIZE OF CITY BLOCKS BURNING FOSSIL FUELS AROUND THE CLOCK. THERE ARE THOUSANDS WORLDWIDE.
"WHEN ONE BURNS OUT, TWO MORE FALL FROM THE SKY. GIFTS FROM YOUR SOLAR COUNCIL."

EVENTUALLY THE EARTH'S TEMPERATURE WILL RISE HIGH ENOUGH TO KILL THE VIRUS.
WE'LL DIE TOO. BUT YOU'LL GET YOUR PLANET BACK.
THAT HAS NOTHING TO DO WITH US, OR THE *BILLIONS* OF INNOCENT PEOPLE THAT STAND TO--

I WOULD SLAUGHTER YOU ALL WITH MY OWN HANDS IF IT SPARED THE LIFE OF JUST *ONE* OF MY PEOPLE.
WE HAVE SUFFERED *ENOUGH*.
YOU SHOULD ALL MAKE YOUR PEACE. THE NEXT TRANSPORT TO THE SURFACE LEAVES IN THE MORNING.
PLEASE...YOU DON'T HAVE TO DO THIS...
YOU WERE PREPARED TO DIE FOR YOUR CAUSE, AGENT CROSS. NOW PREPARE TO DIE...
...FOR MINE.

SOMEWHERE ON SKYBOROUGH.
SNIPP!

ALL IS ARRANGED. THE COLLECTORS WILL COME FOR THE BOY WITHIN THE HOUR.
BRING HIM TO ME.

IT'S TIME, MY YOUNG FRIEND.

TIME FOR YOU TO BEAR OUR STANDARD. TO DO YOUR PART TO END THE TYRANNY OF HUMAN LIFE.
WILL YOU DO THE WORK THAT THE SWORD OF GOD HAS INTENDED FOR YOU?
DO YOU HAVE THE COURAGE, GIAN...
...TO SAVE US FROM OURSELVES?

HOURS LATER.
"COME IN, SPARROW.
"YOU ARE NOT CLEARED TO LAND. AGAIN, YOU ARE *NOT* CLEARED TO LAND."

SPARROW, DO YOU READ?
WHAT'S THE PROBLEM?
IT'S GRANLI AND BLAKE, THE MEN KESTREL LEFT AT SYNGEN STATION.
THEIR SHUTTLE'S ON APPROACH BUT IT ISN'T RESPONDING.

MOVE! MOVE! MOVE!
POSSIBLE HOSTILES INBOUND!

STOP!
HANDS ABOVE YOUR HEAD!
STAY WHERE YOU ARE OR WE WILL OPEN FIRE!

GET ON THE GROUND, SOLDIER!
ON THE GROUND NOW!

YOU HEARD THE MAN, ASSHOLE. ON THE--!

DEEET DEEET
DEEEEEET

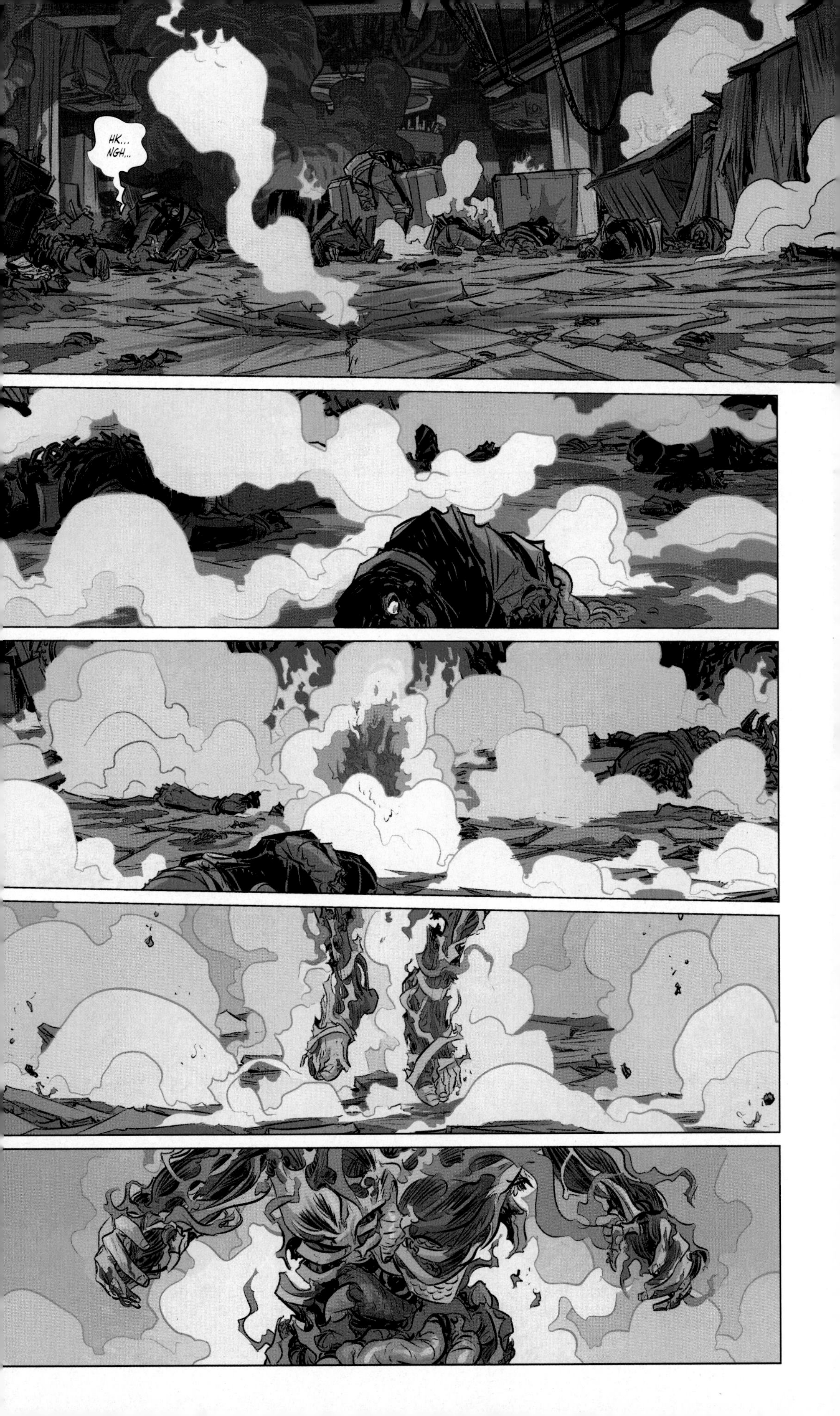
HK... NGH...

BRUTAL NOODLES
ENJOY
HAVE A BRUTAL DAY

5

WARNING.
SECURITY BREACH.
SKYBOROUGH.
WARNING.
SECURITY BREACH.
WARNING.
SECURITY BREACH.
REGI FOR THE WIN.

WE HAVE TO GET YOU OUT OF HERE.
WHAT'S GOING ON?
A CONSTRUCT IN THE EASTERN HANGAR.
15
SEAL OFF THE AREA AND EXTERMINATE IT.
KESTREL...
WE FEED OUR PEOPLE TO THE VIRUS TO KEEP IT ON THE SURFACE. IF WE STOP, IT WILL COME FOR US HERE.
WE AREN'T GOING ANYWHERE, VAGER.
NOT UNTIL WE SEE THIS THROUGH.
EYES FRONT!
NO STOPPING!

HNG!
I SAID NO STOPPING!
SO DID YOU DO IT?
PREPARE TO DIE.
DO WHAT?
NOPE. YOU?
NAH...
VRRRR
THOOM!!
DAMN! THEY'VE ALREADY LEFT!

COME ON, NATHAN... *THINK!*
CROSS WOULD KNOW WHAT TO DO.
WHEN IT COMES TO PLANS SHE'S THE--

DISCO QUEEN

TEN OLYMPUS AVE.
TRAGEDY IN DOWNTOWN THARSIS TODAY AFTER A SUICIDE BOMBER TOOK THE LIVES OF OVER A HUNDRED PEOPLE.
AUTHORITIES CONFIRM THAT THE SWORD OF GOD HAS CLAIMED RESPONSIBILITY.
KING NEWS

HOW LONG BEFORE THE MEDIA CALLS OUR BLUFF?
HARD TO SAY.
GET ZANE ON THE LINE.

MADAM PRESIDENT! I CAN'T THANK YOU ENOUGH FOR THIS OPPORTUNITY! *WHAT A PRODUCTION!*
LIKE TO SEE THE *FILM ACADEMY* IGNORE ME NOW! HAHA! NOT THAT THEY WOULD EVER FIND OUT BUT *WHEN THEY DO--!*
THANK YOU FOR ALL YOUR HARD WORK, MR. FERONI. ARCADIA IS IN YOUR DEBT.

BEEP
MADAM PRESIDENT, CONGRATULATIONS ON A SUCCESSFUL--
SAVE IT, ZANE. IF YOU HAD YOUR DRUTHERS THE VICTIMS WOULD HAVE BEEN *ALIVE* WHEN WE BLEW THEM UP.
WHAT DID WE LEARN FROM DJINN?
WHAM

WE CAN CONFIRM THAT JENNER HAS A PSYCHIC OF HIS OWN. ONE FAR MORE POWERFUL THAN ANY SERVING ARCADIA.
AN ASSUMPTION WE'VE BEEN WORKING UNDER FOR SOME TIME NOW GIVEN THAT OUR INFILTRATION ATTEMPTS KEEP FAILING.
WHERE'S JENNER?

ACCORDING TO DJINN, HE'S ON VENUS, NEAR A BORDER TOWN CALLED "HERA'S HOPE."
WHERE SPECIFICALLY?
WELL... OUR WORKING THEORY IS THAT--

YOU HAVE NO IDEA, DO YOU.
WE'RE GETTING CLOSER. AND WE'VE ACQUIRED A HANDFUL OF DETAILS REGARDING FUTURE SMALL-SCALE--
END CALL.

FUUUUCK!!

COUNCILMAN CYRUS...YES...
I'VE RECONSIDERED MY POSITION ON THE THERMAL DROPS.
YOU CAN HAVE MY VOTE TO CONTINUE THEM.
BUT I NEED SOMETHING FROM YOU...
CROSS
AMANDA J.

EEEEEEEEEE!
RUN!
HELP US!

PACE! WHERE DO WE GO?!
I DON'T KNOW! THERE'S TOO MANY!
MAYBE THIS WAY?!

OOPS.

BANG!

GREAT IDEA, PAST-NATHAN! HOW HARD COULD IT BE TO FLY A *SPACE-TURD?!*
MAN, WHITE LIGHT DOES *NOT* GET ENOUGH CREDIT. NO WONDER SHE THINKS SHE'S SURROUNDED BY...

...ASSHOLES...
OKAY, OPTIONS... CRASH-LAND POSSIBLY KILLING MY FRIENDS IN THE PROCESS *OR*...

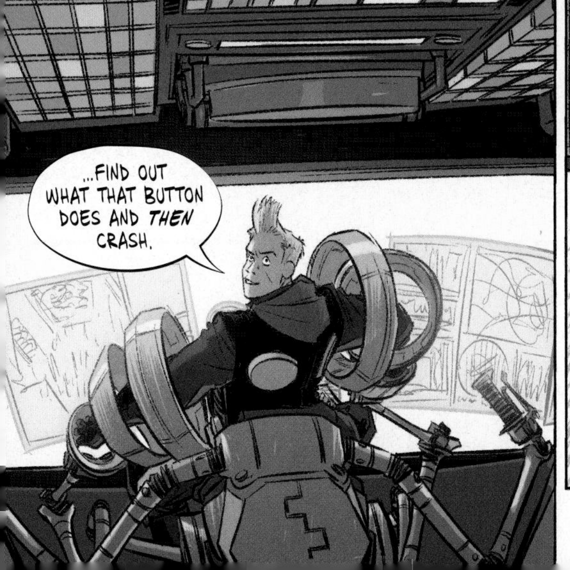
...FIND OUT WHAT THAT BUTTON DOES AND *THEN* CRASH.

I'M TAKIN' DOOR NUMBER TWO!

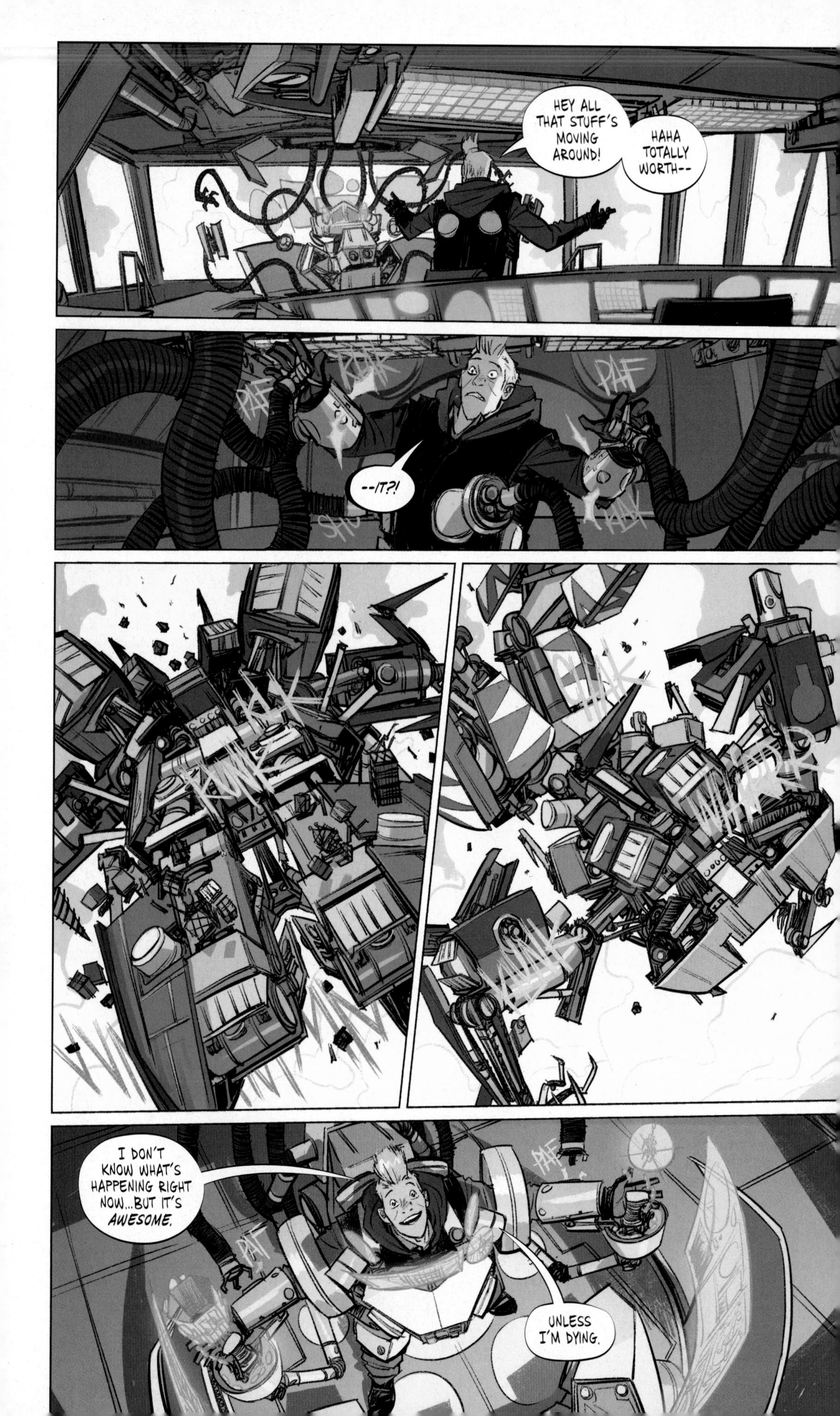
HEY ALL THAT STUFF'S MOVING AROUND!
HAHA TOTALLY WORTH--
PAF
KLAK
PAF
PAF
--IT?!
I DON'T KNOW WHAT'S HAPPENING RIGHT NOW...BUT IT'S *AWESOME.*
PAF
PAF
UNLESS I'M DYING.

THEY'RE COMING!
STAY TOGETHER!

I AM DOING THIS!
NATHAN...?

FIRE, FIRE... I NEED...
...FIRE!
FIRE
I THINK I USED IT ALL! HURRY!
I HAVE NO IDEA WHAT I'M DOING!

HEY, YOU'RE INSIDE ME!
THAT CAME OUT WRONG.
NATHAN! HOW THE HELL DID--?
WELL AFTER YOU WERE TAKEN I WAS KIND OF IN A BAD PLACE.
"BUT THEN I GOT AN IDEA!
"THE SOLDIERS KESTREL TOLD TO STAY BEHIND HAD LEFT THEIR TRANSPORT UNGUARDED.
"SO I STOLE IT, FLEW TO ARGUS'S LAB, AND TOLD REGI I'D FREE HIM IF HE HELPED ME FREE YOU. THEN WE HAD MILK AND COOKIES."
"WAIT, YOU... WHAT?!"
TINK
"I KNOW, RIGHT?! ARGUS ACTUALLY HAD MILK AND COOKIES!"

YEAH, FOR A HYBRID VIRUS-MAN REGI'S GREAT. HE UNDERSTANDS MORE THAN ARGUS THINKS HE DOES.
HE DID MUNCH ON MY ARM HAIR AT ONE POINT THOUGH, AND THAT WAS WEIRD.
RIGHT, WELL, STRAP IN. WE'RE NOT DONE YET.

TWERK
WERK
TERK

IS SHE--?
SNIFF
I'M SO PROUD...

I KNEW YOUR FATHER, YOU KNOW.

MERO WAS A STRONG MAN. A PASSIONATE MAN.
YOU REMIND ME OF HIM.
BUT I CAN SEE THAT YOU ARE AFRAID.

DON'T WORRY, GIAN.
IT WILL ALL BE OVER--

NOW.

COLLISION IMMINENT.

HALF THE VIRUS'S FOOD JUST EXPLODED.
EVACUATE THE CITY.
WHAT?! YOU WANT TO--

IT'S OVER.

GAH!
WHAT'S HAPPENING?!
I THINK WE MADE IT HANGRY...

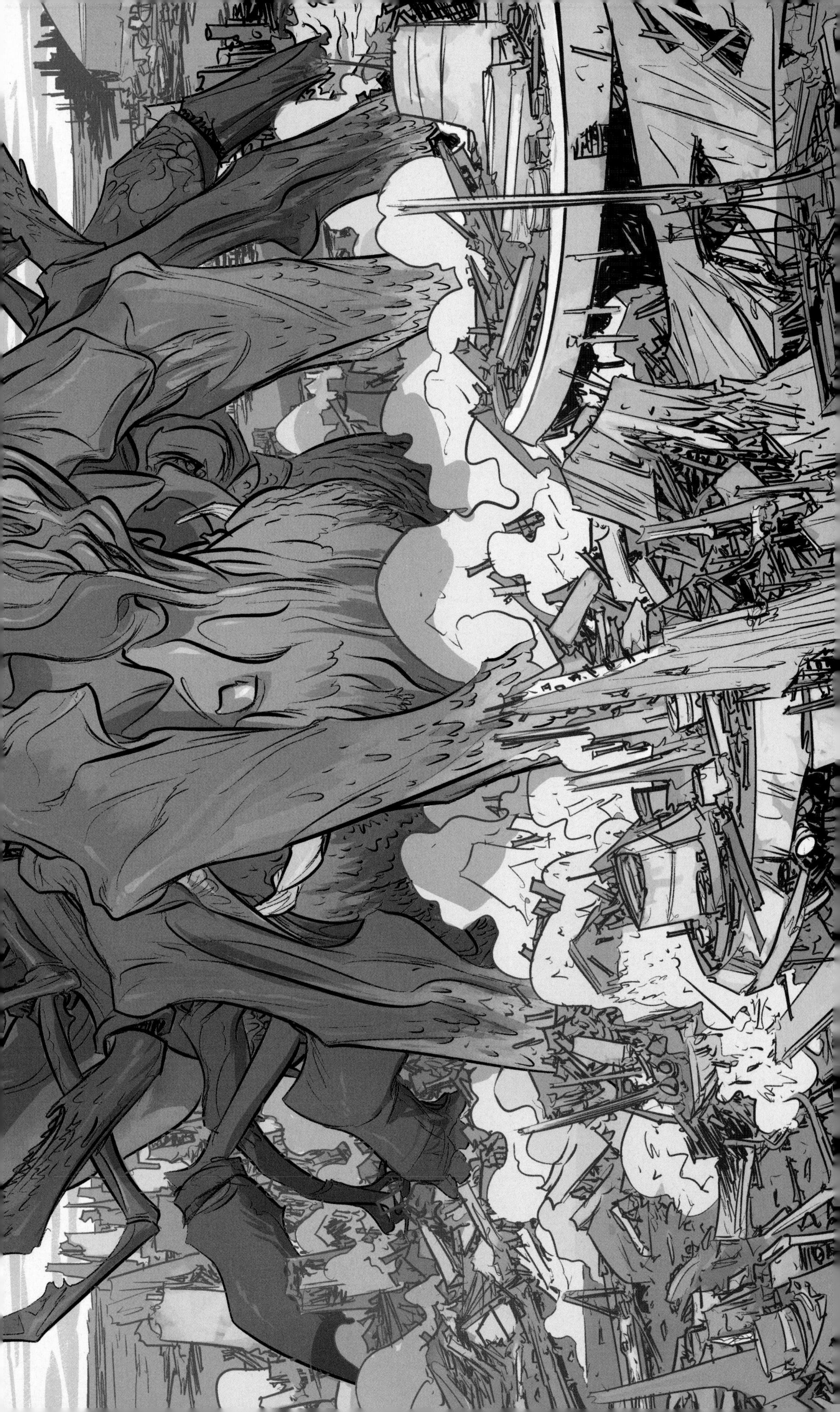

CITIZENS OF SKYBOROUGH...
...PROCEED TO THE NEAREST HANGAR FOR IMMEDIATE EVACUATION.
WHAT DO WE DO NOW?
CROSS?

BEEP
KLAK
KLAK
PAK
KA-BOOM
NYAAAARGH!
TWOOSH
AAAAAGHHH!

WHERE ARE YOU GOING?!
WE AREN'T LEAVING WITHOUT THAT MEMORY DRIVE.
IT COULD BE *ANYWHERE!* LIKE TRYING TO FIND A NEEDLE IN A THOUSAND HAYSTACKS!
CROSS...
IT'S GONE.
WE'LL FIND ANOTHER WAY.

I'VE BEEN WAITING FOR YOU MY WHOLE LIFE.
SO COME ON THEN.
TOK
SKREEEE
COME ON!
MERO...

BOOM
WE CAN'T TAKE MANY MORE!

HELP!
DON'T LEAVE ME HERE!
SKREEEEEEEEE!
LET'S GO BEFORE THAT THING DESTROYS THE CITY!
WAIT!

GIVE ME YOUR HAND!
PLEASE!
YOU COULD SAVE US!
YOU COULD SAVE HUMANITY!
"I KNOW THIS HURTS."
SSKREEEEEEEEEE
NO!

BRUTAL
NOODLES
ENJOY
HAVE A
BRUTAL
DAY

FWEEEEEE
EEEE

SURPRISE!
WHAT ARE YOU--?
WE'RE CELEBRATING! WHITE LIGHT BAKED YOU A CAKE!
WHITE LIGHT HATES ME.

OH, A HUNDRED PERCENT.
YOU SHOULD DEFINITELY *NOT* EAT THAT CAKE.
NATHAN!
STOP.

THE MEMORY DRIVE IS *GONE!*
WHAT EXACTLY DO YOU THINK HAPPENS NOW, *HUH?!*
YOU GO BACK TO GETTING *"CLEVER WITH THE WEATHER"?!* SHAKING YOUR ASS WHILE *REAL* PEOPLE *DIE?!*

NO MEMORY DRIVE MEANS OUR MISSION IS A *FAILURE.* IT MEANS WE HAVE *NO* BARGAINING CHIP FOR GETTING OFF EARTH.
IT MEANS WE'RE *ALL DEAD.*

SO I HAVE *ZERO* INTEREST IN WHATEVER IT IS *YOU'RE* SO HAPPY AB--

IAN BLACK

WHAT? HOW DID YOU--? WHERE DID--?
GRABBED IT BEFORE KESTREL'S SOLDIERS COULD.
I'VE BEEN HOLDING ONTO IT BECAUSE...
I WASN'T SURE WANTED TO GIVE IT TO YOU.
I THOUGHT A LOT ABOUT LEAVING IT BEHIND.
EVEN THOUGHT ABOUT TAKING MY LIFE.
BUT... MOSTLY I THOUGHT ABOUT HIM.
WHAT WAS HE LIKE?
WHY DID HE DO WHAT HE DID?
WHERE DID I COME FROM?
MAYBE I'M HIS SHOT AT A LIFE HE DIDN'T DESERVE.
MAYBE I'M HIS CHANCE TO BE BETTER, TO DO SOME GOOD BEFORE THE END.
BUT WHAT MATTERS NOW ARE THE CHOICES I MAKE.
AND EVEN THOUGH I CAN'T MAKE UP FOR WHAT HE DID...
...I CHOOSE...

...TO DIE TRYING.
I...I DON'T KNOW WHAT TO SAY...
HOW ABOUT YOU'VE ALWAYS FOUND ME INCREDIBLY ATTRACTIVE AND HAD CIRCUMSTANCES BEEN DIFFERENT...

NATHAN...
JOKES.
C'MON...

WHATTA YA SAY WE GO SAVE THE SOLAR SYSTEM?

YES! EARTH-SIDE! WE'RE BACK, BABY!
DON'T YOU SCREW THIS UP FOR ME, CETH. CORPORAL'S GIVEN US ANOTHER CHANCE SO NO MORE FIRING AT OUR OWN SHIPS.
THEY ALL LOOK THE SAME!
SSH! KEEP YOUR VOICE DOWN!
LAST THING WE NEED IS THE CORPORAL HEARING YOUR TRIGGER-HAPPY ASS ON SOME "THEY ALL LOOK THE SAME!"
THEY DO NOT LOOK THE SAME.
HEY, UH...ISN'T THAT THE SHIP THAT CRASHED THROUGH THE--
GIMME THAT, YOU--
OH CRAP!

WHERE ARE THE SURVIVORS?
SETTLED IN THE CARGO HOLD. BUT AIN'T NONE OF US GONNA LAST LONG AGAINST THAT BARRICADE 'LESS YOU KNOW SOMETHIN' I DON'T.
JUST LET ME DO THE TALKING.

UMMM...
IS THAT...?
PROB'LY A DIFFERENT CAKE.

RIGHT.

UNIDENTIFIED CRAFT, YOU ARE TRAVELING IN A QUARANTINE ZONE. POWER DOWN OR WE WILL ENGAGE, OVER.

DEET
THIS IS AMANDA CROSS. I'M AN ARCADIAN INTELLIGENCE FIELD AGENT. MY CREDENTIALS ARE BEING TRANSFERRED VIA SECURE CHANNEL.
IT'S CRITICAL THAT I SPEAK WITH ADMIRAL DAX AS SOON AS--
AGENT CROSS...

THIS IS PRESIDENT BURGA.
I THINK IT'S TIME FOR US TO HAVE A LITTLE CHAT.

TWO HOURS LATER.

THAT'S QUITE A STORY.
UNFORTUNATELY WE HAVE A ZERO-TOLERANCE POLICY FOR INDIVIDUALS THAT HAVE BEEN EXPOSED TO THE VIRUS.
WHAT ABOUT A RENLY SCAN? IT CAN DETECT THE VIRUS AT THE ATOMIC LEVEL.

THAT'S CLASSIFIED. IT'S ALSO EXPERIMENTAL, EXCRUCIATING, AND ASTRONOMICALLY EXPENSIVE.
HOWEVER...GIVEN YOUR CIRCUMSTANCES, I'VE MADE ARRANGEMENTS FOR THE SOLAR COUNCIL TO ALLOW THE SCAN AND RELEASE OF YOU AND YOUR TEAM.
PROVIDED YOU COME IN.
AND THE SURVIVORS?

THEY CAN LIVE OUT THEIR LIVES ON A QUARANTINE VESSEL, OR THEY CAN RETURN TO EARTH.
HOW DO I KNOW I CAN TRUST YOU?
TRUSTING EACH OTHER IS A RISK WE BOTH HAVE TO TAKE.

WHAT ABOUT NATHAN?
MR. BRIGHT WILL BE OVERWRITTEN IMMEDIATELY AFTER YOUR TEAM IS CLEARED.

WHAT IS IT?

HE THINKS THE SWORD OF GOD HAS THE OTHER SAMPLE.
I HAD THE OTHER SAMPLE DESTROYED WHEN I TOOK OFFICE. YOUR DEPARTMENT WAS BRIEFED AS I RECALL.
I NEEDED TO MOTIVATE HIM.

I'LL PASS THAT ALONG.
CONGRATULATIONS, AGENT CROSS.

"WELL DONE."

WE AIN'T GETTIN' ON NO GOVERNMENT SHIP!

RELAX! IT'S ALL ARRANGED. YOU'RE WITH ME NOW.
HOW DO WE KNOW THEY'LL HONOR THEIR END OF THE DEAL?

YOU WANNA GET EVEN, MARSHAL, THIS IS THE PATH YOU WALK. WE GET DOUBLE-CROSSED, BY ALL MEANS KILL EVERYONE ON BOARD THAT SHIP. HELL, I'LL HELP YOU.
BUT UNTIL THAT HAPPENS, I NEED BOTH OF YOU FOCUSED AND READY FOR WHAT'S COMING.

WE'VE MADE IT THIS FAR TOGETHER.

I WON'T ABANDON YOU.

SYNGEN STATION.
THE ARCTIC CIRCLE.

FWOOM!

Piiiii-cKLLLES!
WHERE ARE YOU, FUZZY-FACE?!

OOOF!
HAHA!
I MISSED YOU TOO!

BIG BABY.

THE PRESIDENT'S CRUISER.
THREE DAYS LATER.
I DON'T KNOW HOW YOU'RE EATING RIGHT NOW.
I'M STILL NAUSEOUS FROM THE SCAN.
HOW'S THE FOOD?
OH, *UH*...GOOD, I GUESS. THE BRUTAL BOWLS BACK ON REDD BAY ARE BETTER BUT...
...NOT BAD FOR A LAST MEAL.
AGENT CROSS? IT'S TIME.
BRUTAL NOODLES

WELL, AGENT CROSS...
IT WAS NICE KNOWIN' YOU.
THANK YOU.

--TWO SETS OF NEURAL CIRCUITS IN THE SYNAPTO-DENDRITIC NET, ONE TO STORE THE MEMORY AND THE OTHER TO RETRIEVE IT.
BASIC PRINCIPLES OF HOLONOMIC BRAIN THEORY. WHERE'D YOU GO TO--GIMME THAT!
BLORCH
DAMNED RENLY SCANS.
HE'S HERE, DOCTOR. ARE YOU READY?
DO I LOOK READY? JUST ERP PUT HIM IN THE CHAIR.
MAKE SURE THOSE RESTRAINTS ARE SECURE.
NO TELLING WHAT KIND OF MOOD THE SUBJECT WILL BE IN ONCE THE SWITCH IS MADE.
MMMMMM

OKAY...

DO IT.

HRKK
KLATCH
NO...
WAIT!

BLOODY HELL!
WHAT'S HAPPENING?! WHY ARE WE STOPPING?!
DOCTOR ARGUS...
...WE HAVE A PROBLEM.
EMERGENCY SHUT DOWN
A BULLET?
LODGED IN THE CHASSIS OF THE MEMORY DRIVE. THAT'S CORRECT.
AND WE'RE JUST FINDING OUT ABOUT THIS NOW BECAUSE...?
I DID ASK FOR MORE TIME.
LOVELY.
WELL...
...ANY OTHER IDEAS BEFORE I ORDER YOU ALL KILLED?

WE SEND MR. BRIGHT IN.

YOU WANT TO SEND...A *WEATHERMAN*...TO INFILTRATE THE SWORD OF GOD?
NOT A WEATHERMAN... *IAN BLACK*. WE SEND THE PRODIGAL SON HOME.

ARE YOU OUT OF YOUR MIND?
NATHAN IS *HARDLY IAN BLACK*.
HE WILL BE BY THE TIME WE'RE THROUGH WITH HIM.
OUR VIRTUAL CONDITIONING AND COGNITIVE IMPLANTS HAVE IMPROVED SINCE OU LAST INFILTRATION ATTEMPT.
WE HAVE EVERY REASON TO BELIEVE OUR NEX ONE WILL BE A SUCCESS.

MADAM PRESIDENT!
YOU NEED TO SEE THIS...

9:23:57:49
TEN DAYS...?

JARED, IS THAT WHAT I THINK IT IS?
SOME KIND OF COUNTDOWN.
THE SWORD OF GOD IS BROADCASTING IT SYSTEM-WIDE.
PEOPLE ARE STARTING TO PANIC. WE NEED TO ADDRESS THEM AS SOON AS POSSIBLE.

YOU HAVE A WEEK TO TURN NATHAN BRIGHT INTO A MONSTER.

HEAVEN HELP US IF YOU FAIL.

SOON.
KLATCH
WELL?
HE'S IN.
SAYS HE'LL DO WHATEVER HE HAS TO DO.
WHAT ABOUT HIS MIND?
SNAP!
HE'S PRETTY FRIED, BUT ARGUS SAYS HE SHOULD RECOVER.
THINK WE CAN GET HIM THERE IN TIME?
WHEN WE'RE FINISHED, HE SHOULDN'T HAVE ANY PROBLEM CASUALLY PASSING FOR IAN BLACK.
THE REAL SONG AND DANCE HAPPENS WHEN HE ENCOUNTERS THEIR PSYCHIC.
HER READING OF HIS MIND WILL TRIGGER A BLOCK OF VIRTUAL MEMORIES, EXPLAINING WHAT MR. BLACK HAS BEEN UP TO THE PAST SEVEN YEARS.
KLATCH
WHERE'D WE LEARN T TRICK?

THE PEARL'S FANTASY MURDER TECH. REMARKABLE WHAT HIS PEOPLE ACCOMPLISHED.
HOW WILL HE COMMUNICATE WITH US ONCE HE'S INSIDE?
HE WON'T HAVE TO. WE'LL HEAR WHAT HE HEARS...SEE THE WORLD THROUGH HIS EYES.
"A WIRE? WON'T THEY BE ABLE TO DETECT--?"
"NOT CONVENTIONALLY. THESE NEW TRANSMITTERS ARE A HUNDRED PERCENT ORGANIC."
I JUST HOPE WE CAN PULL THIS OFF.
IF WE DON'T, HE'S DEAD. AND LIKELY SO ARE WE.
EITHER WAY, HE AND ALL HIS FRIENDS WILL BE BURNING IN HELL.
"THAT'S ALL THE HOPE I NEED."

ONE WEEK LATER.

"DAMN VENUSIAN STORMS.

"WE'VE LOST VISUAL!

"WE'RE OKAY. SIGNAL'S COMING BACK."

BANG!

PIECE OF SHIT DIDN'T EVEN FLINCH.
OH MY GOD...DID HE JUST--?
WHAT'D YOU EXPECT?

I--I DON'T KNOW...I...
THIS IS WHAT WE WANTED. HE'LL BE TRUSTED NOW.

SORRY TO INTERRUPT, BUT I NEED A WORD.
CLEAR THE LINE, ARGUS!

"I'M AFRAID IT CAN'T WAIT."

"WE'VE MANAGED TO DECODE THE MEMORY DRIVE.
"WE FOUND A--"

"WE'RE PAST THAT NOW, DOCTOR."

"THEY'RE MOVING HIM."
"YOU DON'T UNDERSTAND.
"LISTEN..."

THIS IS DR. MIRIAM NYSETH. APRIL 19TH, 2763 REGARDING CASE NUMBER 35A749.
"DESPITE NUMEROUS EFFORTS, SUBJECT IAN BLACK'S MIND HAS RESISTED MEMORIAL SEIZURE.
"NO FURTHER PROGRESS IS POSSIBLE WITHOUT RISKING IRREPARABLE DAMAGE TO THE BRAIN.
"ALL ATTEMPTS TO WIPE THE SUBJECT'S MEMORY HAVE FAILED.
"I REPEAT..."

WELCOME BACK.

"...THE MEMORY WIPE HAS FAILED."

TO BE CONCLUDED...

BRUTAL
NOODLES
ENJOY
HAVE A BRUTAL DAY

Cover by Nathan Fox

The Weatherman.™

Jody LeHeup
Nathan Fox
Moreno Dinisio

$3.99 US
Vol. 2

2

image

Cover by Nathan Fox

The Weather Man.™

Jody LeHeup
Nathan Fox
Moreno Dinisio

$3.99 US
Vol. 2

3

Cover by Nathan Fox

The Weather Man.™

Jody LeHeup
Nathan Fox
Moreno Dinisio

$3.99 US
Vol. 2

4

image

The Weather Man.™
Jody LeHeup
Nathan Fox
Moreno Dinisio
$3.99 US
Vol. 2
5

Cover by Nathan Fox

The Weather Man.™

Jody LeHeup
Nathan Fox
Moreno Dinisio

$3.99 US
Vol. 2

6

image

Cover by Nathan Fox

Vol. 2 #1 Variant by Andrew Robinson

Vol. 2 #2 Variant by Andrew Robinson

Vol. 2 #3 Variant by Andrew Robinson

#4 Variant by Andrew Robinson

Vol. 2 #5 Variant by Andrew Robinson

Vol. 2 #6 Variant by Andrew Robinson

Vol. 2 #2 Variant by Mike Mignola and Dave Stewart

Vol. 2 #3 Variant by Stephanie Hans

Vol. 2 #5 Variant by Daniel Warren Johnson and Mike Spicer

Vol. 2 #4 Variant by Jason Pearson

Vol. 2 #1 Variant by Duncan Fegredo

Vol. 2 #[illegible] Variant by José Ladrönn

Vager
Kestrel
Royd Filbert
Dr. Argus

Zane
Pickles
Pace

CREATURE CONCEPT 1
FLY EYES
SPIDER EYES
MANDIBLE &
TEETH

T-REX
GORILLA
SPIDER.
EYES
FLY EYES ON
SIDE OF HEAD
Concept Art by Nathan Fox

CREATURE CONCEPT 2

TRANSLUCENT HEAD/BRAIN STUFF.

NORMAL
CLOSED

VAMPIRE SQUID SHAPE.

MAD
OPEN

CRAB-LIKE ARMS (6 TOTAL)

LONG BEAR LIKE CLAWS.

MINI TENTACLES.

Concept Art by Nathan Fox

TENTACLES.
STANDING
UPRIGHT
DEEP SEA
MASHUP.

Pin-up by Nathan Fox

Jody LeHeup

is the writer and co-creator of the IMAGE COMICS series THE WEATHERMAN and the co-writer and co-creator of SHIRTLESS BEAR-FIGHTER!. A former editor, Jody edited many titles including UNCANNY X-FORCE, DEADPOOL and STRANGE TALES for MARVEL and QUANTUM AND WOODY for VALIANT. He lives in Queens, New York.

Nathan Fox

is the artist and co-creator of the IMAGE COMICS series THE WEATHERMAN, the artist of DARK REIGN: ZODIAC for MARVEL, and a contributing artist on DMZ from DC/VERTIGO and HAUNT, also from Image. He's the chair and founder of the MFA Visual Narrative program at the School of Visual Arts in New York and a prolific commercial illustrator with clients including Nickelodeon, the *NY Times*, Rockstar Games, Sony, *Esquire*, *Rolling Stone* Magazine, and Apple, among others.

The Weather Man. WILL CONCLUDE IN VOLUME 3!

THE WEATHERMAN Volume 2. First printing. February 2020. Published by Image Comics, Inc. Office of publication: 2701 NW Vaughn St., Ste. 780, Portland, OR 97210. Printed in the USA. For information regarding the CPSIA on this printed material call: 203-595-3636. All inquiries: theweathermancomic@gmail.com. ISBN: 978-1-5343-1503-7.

IMAGECOMICS.COM

All inquiries:
theweathermancomic@gmail.com

WM_Comic